PERMANENT
ERRORS

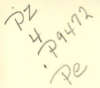
REYNOLDS
PRICE

PERMANENT
ERRORS

NEW YORK
ATHENEUM
1970

Some of these pieces have appeared—in earlier forms—in Esquire, Playboy, Red Clay Reader, Shenandoah, The Southern Review, Vogue; *and the group* LATE WARNINGS *was published in 1969 in a limited edition by the Albondocani Press.*

Library of Congress catalog card number 70–124974
Published simultaneously in Canada by
McClelland and Stewart Ltd
Manufactured in the United States of America by
Kingsport Press, Inc., Kingsport, Tennessee
Designed by Harry Ford
First Edition

FOR

EUDORA WELTY

TO THE READER

Permanent Errors is the title of the book, not of any piece, though it might be the name of each; for despite their gathering over several years and their variance in shape and intent, the pieces share a controlling effort—the attempt to isolate in a number of lives the central error of act, will, understanding which, once made, has been permanent, incurable, but whose diagnosis and palliation are the hopes of continuance.

Not all the pieces are stories, though all are narratives in prose of various gears and gaits and are grouped by kind and concern.

The parts of the first group "Fool's Education" ("The Making of a Fool"? "A Fool's Unmaking"? "From Fool to Sage"?) are independent of one another yet, read in order, form a different larger story. That was the intention—these are not fragments of an unfinishable novel but subaqueous raids on an iceberg's concealment, from which an exposed top may be inferred; thus they lack much of the connective tissue usual in narrative. Nor are they—despite concurrences of place and date—attempts at self-improvement or punishment through autobiography. (The topographic details of "Waiting at Dachau" are fifteen-year-old memories of a visit to the camp, unchecked and now uncheckable since its decoration with monuments, a museum. The statistics of imprisonment and death are drawn from respectable printed sources, including records of the Nuremberg trials, but are subject to the uncertainty and contradiction of all sources on the Final Solution.)

The second group is clearly personal; but none of these is intended as a story—more nearly as poems; narrative poems of personal loss, therefore elegies.

"Truth and Lies," the first piece of the third group, is the first-written of the book and is the most recognizable story of all (though related to the others); but again in "Good and Bad Dreams," the six parts of the whole are both detachable and augmentative—each an independently ambulatory organism but also a contributor to the isolation of a larger error than emerges from the parts.

"Walking Lessons" sums—without that as its purpose—the themes of the others.

There are repetitions (one Sara, one Sarah—different women; three men who are quasi-interchangeable lenses—two of them writers, a typical form of manual work and the one I know closely). The book is, in several ways, a set of variations.

Last, I'm aware of irony in the title—that the pieces are potential errors of my own, fondly engraved in indelible print, hoarded in mineshafts against an End. So, potentially, is any breath drawn.

R. P. *February 1970*

CONTENTS

THE ALCHEMIST

Laughing, the chemist set the hot alembic
Where it could cool, fuming at his grin.
Now he knew what—simply—he would need
To force the thing he coveted to come—

Mind as girdling as the zodiac,
Free and sovereign but fiercely ruled,
Glomerate with power as the sea;
Eons for seething down this crystal crib.

—In which the monster of his yearning lay
(Got now, blind, by him on this blind night),
Prima materia—*rose past him to God;*

While babbling like a drunk, he lay among
His magic-set, his priceless brittle gear,
And craved the crumb of gold he'd just now had.

R. P.   *after Rilke,* Der Alchimist

O N E

FOOL'S EDUCATION

THE HAPPINESS OF OTHERS

THEY killed two hours of the twenty remaining over lunch at the Lamb, chewing each bite as long and mercilessly as though their stomachs held ravenous babies, open-mouthed to suck in the stream of tepid pap. The work of eating also saved them from talk, that and their pretense of fervent eavesdropping on the two other guests as late as they (an apoplectic retired colonel and his, what? daughter? wife?—a colorless moony horse in flowers whose only words when the old man asked "Are you happy?" were "Thank you").

Then when even the colonel had yielded to the waitress's glare of perfect hate—it was half-past two; her life awaited—they finished their coffee and entered the sun, the day like a baby dumped on their doorstep, gorgeous but unwanted, condemning as an angel. And gilding—it made Sara's body seem gold, warm and workable. Even the black hair transmuting quickly, through bronze to gold. They stood a moment—Charles Tamplin seeing that, she knowing he saw it, both knowing its deceit.

She reached for his wrist. He gave her his hand. But she did not take it—"I was looking for the time," she said. He extended his watch. She studied it carefully, returned it to his side, gave him the sum, "Eighteen hours till I rest on the bosom of the deep." They both gave the brief statutory grin—they spoke of her sailing, their permanent parting, in jokes: "The Noble Experiment Ended Smiling"—then stood again, loose. "Where now?" she said.

"The church?" he said.

She nodded, stepped to go. "You can say me the poem. A final performance."

He smiled, bowed slightly, double-stepped to take the lead; and they walked down the High Street, as separate as sisters, to the old stone bridge, short and narrow, at the bottom. She looked right to where the spire stood, tan and clear. But he pointed to the crossroads beyond the bridge, right to Shipton-under-Wychwood, left to Stow-on-the-Wold; vital junction still guarded from Nazis by a pillbox smothered in roses now, its black slot empty, unarmed, unused, shielding only village lovers seized here by urgency or tramps in the rain. They had once crawled into it themselves, been amazed by its neatness—no garbage or excrement but well-pressed earth and a few penciled names.

She smiled, said "Ah-dew," the word she had chosen all week for last views. Then she ran up the loud Windrush to the church.

He gave her the lead, loped behind, in her tracks.

They had been through the church three or four times together; he more often, alone, or with college friends. But they trailed through its dark chill now as if discovering—the Lady chapel defaced by Roundheads, the lead font scratched with the name of a prisoner shot by Cromwell next morning in the yard, the tomb of the barber to Henry VIII; then the small painted bust of Lucius Cary (beside his wife's with her breasts displayed), killed at Newbury, age thirty-three, Viscount Falkland, Lord of Great Tew, friend to Ben Jonson and mourned by him.

Sara touched the bust, its pink features fresh and vapid as a baby's. Then she said with more force than the stillness required, "Any man of thirty with a face bare as this, deserves to die."

"It's the sculptor," he said. "Don't blame poor Cary."

"But I do," she said. "If he'd been half a man, left behind a man's memory, his wife or whoever would have never paid for *this*—" She thumped the smooth forehead; it thudded, all but grunted. "Say his poem anyhow."

Charles Tamplin obeyed, for one line, in a whisper —"*It is not growing like a tree*—" Then refused, clamped shut. *Deserve*, she had said. She did not deserve this. One waste he could spare himself.

In his pause, she prompted; completed the sentence (all she knew of the poem)—"*In bulk, doth make man better be.*" Then she watched him and waited.

He did not face her but he shook his head. She accepted, walked on, so he stood alone and said to himself, slowly and clearly to the walls of his skull, Jonson's ten perfect lines to the memory of Cary—

> *It is not growing like a tree*
> *In bulk, doth make man better be*

Or standing long an oak, three hundred year,
To fall a log at last, dry, bald and sear.
A lily of a day
Is fairer far in May
Although it fall and die that night;
It was the plant and flower of light.
In small proportions, we just beauty see;
And in short measures, life may perfect be.

He felt as though a green leaf uncoiled on his lips.
A kindness to himself, the first for weeks. As though he
might yet survive the scorch, live to tell the tale. What
tale? His and Sara's, the one he knew, only tale there
was. Name another than theirs. Nothing so grand as
betrayal or treason; only the oldest story of all—the
simple entire failure to meet, to serve one another and
delight in the work. Imagine a life of telling that—stories, poems for another fifty years. Well, he could and
must, beginning tomorrow, in eighteen hours. His own
small proportion, just beauty, alone.

When—stronger for the moment of solitude used
—he had wandered toward Sara, past altar and choir,
he found her not in tears nor with her pallor-of-victim
but with head back, eyes wide and fixed on a spot high
above on the crowded wall, the skin of her forehead
and jaw taut with triumph.

"Do you know that?" she said. Not facing him, she
pointed to a marble plaque—*Bartholomew.*

He knew of a house by that name in the village,
but this he had missed—a long inscription. He shook
his head, No, and began to read silently.

"*I found it,*" she said and forced him to listen—

"*Lo, Huddled up together lie*
Gray age, green youth, white infancy.
If death doth nature's laws dispense
And reconciles all difference,
Tis fit one flesh one house should have,
One tomb, one epitaph, one grave;
And they that lived and lovèd either
Should die and lie and sleep together.
Go, reader. Whether go or stay,
Thou must not hence be long away."

He heard her to the end, eyes on her not the
poem. Then he left, half-ran to the south door, the
yard; and had run through half the ruining tombs there
(of wool merchants, stone wool-sacks on each) before
he knew he was fleeing again. He stopped in the light
and, though he did not turn, knew she had not followed, was still inside. Could he leave her there now;
go his own way at last, unexplained, free?—give her all
the time she needed to copy, memorize, digest her
newest triumph; then find her own way to Southamp-
ton, her ship? No. He turned.

She stepped through the south door herself, into
sun; walked briskly to him. "It's better," she said. "It's
a truer poem. It could change whole lives."

He shrugged in a quick gust of wind—still not
spring. "We'll drive toward Shipton," he said. "They
had snow."

So they had—a late flurry, two days before, of
which rare patches clung on in the sun, at the roots of
trees, the lee of walls. As he drove them slowly upward

through the long empty hills, it was all they had to
fasten on—a hunt for snow, like a child's hunt for
lucky white horses to stamp. He would see a white
patch, point it silently to her; she would crane, nod
silently, then find one herself. Time unreeled behind
them, an exhausted ribbon. Then they reached a crest
and rode for a while on its bare bright ridge—not a
flake of snow, not a house, a tree. For half a mile,
Charles Tamplin continued searching, the rising taste
of panic plating his teeth. At last, again, they were
locked alone together. And all his doing, a simple ride
to kill a day as painlessly as possible; and now the
whole world, in conspiracy, had slunk into hiding, leaving him and her, her *on* him, no escape, no choice, only
needs to face, their airless symbiosis to swallow, their
sentence to accept.

But she did not speak, continued searching too; so
the panic leeched away and he felt alone, not with her
but with her story, hers and his—this very day a well-
shaped story itself. Their neutral lunch, his victory over
her at Cary's bust, her excited discovery of a mass-epi-
taph, his moment of flight and now this ride which
would last on till dusk, bring them down silently from
the hills into Woodstock—a walk by the darkening
lake at Blenheim (the lake sliding through a whole
gallery of painters with each moment's change of light
—Corot, Monet, Manet, Courbet), supper at The
Bear, then Oxford, separate sleep; in the morning a
calm end. He drove now mechanically, no longer looking, seeing only the shape of that story, lean, rounded.
A small sad proportion, short measure, but beautiful.
He was smiling slightly. He was healing. Safe.

"*Look*," she said.

He looked, straight ahead, hit the brake, barely stopped them. A flock of tan sheep filled the road, buffed his fenders.

"My god," she said. "You nearly killed us."

He winced, invisibly, at her automatic *us* (women had invented the first-person-plural: when *we* got our doctorate; when *we* were in the army); but the whole offered sight was compensation. The stalled car straddled a narrow road. The road was the spine of the highest hill. Sides sloped away quickly onto milder hills, green and gold prospects hung like flats, "effects" in a nineteenth-century play—villages, towers, warrens of life. Sheep filled the road before him and were aiming rightward through a breeched stone wall down the sinking slope. Grass seemed no greener there than where they had left, browner in fact; and a squat bare fruit tree was all the shade. But that seemed their aim —why? "To see the other side"?

They crossed on another half-minute or so, rising from the left, eyeing skittishly the car, but bent all the same on their profitless choice, as though south Ireland lay yards away, sweet green to their knees. Then a black dog shot up, a harassed sergeant, smartening his line, butting, nosing in furious silence—or was it? The car-glass excluded all noise, all sense but vision.

Charles Tamplin felt himself suspended, space and time. This might as easily be Galilee as Oxfordshire, before Christ, before green hills burnt to sand.

And with the last sheep—mostly new slow lambs —a shepherd rose. Young himself and slow—maybe fourteen, red-haired, a credible David, a stick in his right hand which hung loose, languid, oblivious to his flock. As he hopped the shallow ditch, stepped into the

road, he might have been awakened that instant by
warmth, drawn from sleep under leaves by sun, the
melted snow. His eyes squinted sleepily; his face,
hands, clothes seemed fresh with dirt of a hibernation.
He took less notice of the car than his sheep, passed an
arm's reach from it, never flickered a glance. Only—at
the last moment of his profile—he faltered a step,
cocked his chin as though listening but to something
ahead, in his own slow path. Another sound Charles
Tamplin strained to hear, balked by glass. Yet though
the road was clear now, he did not move, to crank the
car or speak; for the shepherd had reached the bare
fruit tree and—his sheep gone on—bent now and
reached to the ground at its roots where a patch of
snow no larger than a plate had survived both sun and
the trampling flock. Now he stood, faced round, ate a
handful of snow, rubbed the rest on his eyes, smiled—
awake now and quick—quite clearly to Sara, said a
word to her, waved. His lips had said "Sorry."

Sara smiled in return, nodding pardon to him
happily.

He took it, waved again, then ran with his dog out
of sight down the slope.

Charles Tamplin looked to Sara—the back of her
head. She still watched the boy—or the space where
he'd stood and staged his grace as natural as breath. She
was gone now, a foot away, still here beside him but
gone for good. There were other doors. She had seen
that at last. Had opened one at least—and shut another.
The crown of her black hair stood now against him, the
thickest gate, barred, guarded, perilous. He cranked the
engine, shifted gear quietly. She still faced the bare
tree, the uneaten snow; so Charles Tamplin thought

they could move on now toward the end of the day, tired and calm. But the wheels had not rolled one turn before he knew—clearly and from her, as though her hidden eyes had flung it backward, a vise for his heart —that the day, the story, ended here, not before or later; ended with the happy boy's word, with Sara's smile; an end but a door blown fiercely open on a world, older, simpler, deeper than he'd known. A family huddled together in death, a handful of snow in early spring light, a "Sorry" through glass, a smiling pardon. Small proportion?—gigantic perhaps, crushing, stifling but just and most beautiful, a possible tale, a possible *life*, secret extended to all but him. Yet *tale*, *life*, *secret* which it now must be his duty to describe, celebrate, adore at a distance. The happiness of others. He adored them through tears.

But Blenheim now, dinner, sleepless night, their final day.

A DOG'S DEATH

I HAD watched the ship leave—and among waving hundreds, one still passenger—at ten that morning, prompt and smooth as a Swiss railway. And it did seem to slide on rails not water—unpitted, firm, two-way, returnable—though it moved toward the winter Atlantic on a trip which would never return to me at least. Then I had driven home dangerously, courting a sharper permanent pain, my conscious destination being bed, drowned sleep. Home was one rented room in the house of a childless working couple —brown walls—and I reached it by noon, fell fully clothed on my narrow bed, flung myself onto sleep like a bale. Sleep took me—as it always kindly has—held me dreamless, careless, alone but not lonely till knocking reached me wherever I lay. I have always waked as quickly as slept, and as desperately—each nerve instantly flayed and clanging—so I was on my feet and moving before I knew what the noise was or where.

Only the knuckles of a hand on my door, a voice —"Mr. Tamplin?"

My landlady—home. Why home at this hour? I glanced to the window, the sky—gray of course but not late, not evening. "Coming," I said and opened on her face; said "Oh," helpless, at what she had become since breakfast—her skin ribbed and thin as cigarette paper, whiter even; hennaed curls collapsed and clinging to her skull, a monstrous child; her eyes red; lips drawn; long neck corded by the effort to speak.

She said, "I am sorry. You were sleeping, I know, on troubles of your own but help me ple—" Her throat refused her.

I waited till she had control again; but when her lips moved they were silent, only flapped—a rain-soaked flag. So I said "Oh I'll live" to her opening apology, smiled, went on—"What's the trouble, Bett?"

She began and found she could manage, but slowly. "Mr. Tamplin, I meant not to worry you, know-ing you have your own heartache. I told Buck this morning when he said you'd help, 'Buck, he's low himself. We won't tell *him* till it's over and done and the flowers planted. We must face it ourselves.'" She stopped, looked over the stairwell rail. "But she's down there now and we can't face it. Not after twelve years."

I honestly did not understand. "Face who? Face what?"

"Her," she said. She stabbed with a finger down again. "The lady vet. She's come for old Peter."

"What's happened to Peter?"

Again she was silenced, stared struggling at me. (Peter was their dog, a low white Sealyham; had been theirs all his life—twelve years—was half-blind now but still, I thought, as strong as a trap. Not a week before, I had entered the front door late at night—on Peter in the hall, lurching on stump legs but galvanized by my sound and smell. He had charged, bare teeth that could pierce a boot. I had dodged, he had lunged—a small

rhino—missed me, struck the wall, fallen. I had made
it safely to the dark front lounge, another joke on Peter,
Bett laughing behind me as she came to retrieve him.)

But she won at last and said, "Tumors. All over.
He's chocked with tumors. I found the first one four
days ago when he wouldn't eat. I was feeling his soft
throat"—she felt her own—"when I found this bird's
egg in there, slipping out of my touch. Then I felt him
all over. They had beat me to him—everywhere, little
sliding eggs. For three days I didn't say a word to Buck
nor you—I knew you faced your own separations—but
I fed Peter what he would eat, sweet chocolate. Still
he's failed every day. Wouldn't move this morning so
Buck went to pet him and felt for himself. They had
grown half-again as big in that time. He went to the
vet, paid her extra money to come to the house. She's
just now looked and says it's hopeless, nothing but
pain. We must put him down, the only kind thing—
she must; *we* can't."

I said, "I'll miss not having him to dodge."

"That's it," she said. "He didn't take to you. Nothing personal though. Never took to anyone but me
and Buck. He'd have torn that vet's hand off by now if
he wasn't so weak. What I'm asking is, why I've waked
you is—since you and him never got along, would you
go now and be with him when she puts him down?"

I had said "Yes" before I thought of a reason—it
would wrench my mind off me awhile, a chance to
begin a life again.

She went down two of the steps, called "Buck."
Out of sight, he opened their parlor door. She said,
"You come here with me. He's coming."

Buck said "All right" and I went down past her,
pressing to the wall not to touch her body—any part of

her, clothing, hair—pressed past Buck also as he climbed toward her, paused, said to me, "It'll only be a moment. Quite painless, she says. But you're very kind."

I nodded but did not say a word. No word, no touch. This new chance had its own rules, cold as glass.

Peter lay in his circle of wicker basket on a bed-pillow covered with a clean white case. His upward eye was open, black, on guard toward the woman, the vet on a hassock beside him; it flicked to me as I entered and said my name; and with recognition he rose in front on two legs, but silently.

I waited, hand on door, for his verdict—enemy breaching his citadel or final friend.

He only looked downward—no other move, no growl, no teeth.

"Come in," she said firmly—a large woman in her late forties, bobbed hair—then softer, "Did you shut the door tightly?"

I nodded Yes, still pressed against it.

"There is really no use your being here—nothing for you to do, that is. Simplest job I ever perform—simplest in the world—but they wanted a witness. Of my kindness perhaps. I *am* kind," she said and raised (not flourished) her large right hand which poised in the air, an elaborate claw composed of her fingers and a hypodermic—middle-sized, plunger drawn on a column of air.

I nodded comprehension.

But she had her own rite to perform, her defense to build—before only me though she spoke it to Peter as she kneaded his chest with her empty hand. "The kindness is not what I do but when—not whether to kill; *when* to kill, you see."

The last had not been put as a question; but again I nodded, as sanction now of her motive and act.

The claw moved swiftly toward its job.

I said "No."

She looked to me stunned, her fine hand balked three inches from Peter. Her lips said *"No?"* in genuine fear. I had questioned her life, defied her defense. "He is not yours," she said. "I have orders from them."

Before her fear became anger, I said, "I must do my part." My part, I saw, was to stand nearer in. I took the steps, stood a foot from Peter—he was still half-risen, watching his feet. I said "All right."

The claw flew toward a taut space she had stretched with two free fingers in Peter's chest. The needle popped as it tore the rind. Her thumb pumped downward for three steady seconds, every atom of air.

Peter buckled on his legs, fell forward on his pillow. He had never looked up, shown surprise or coughed.

She breathed and began to stroke his ear. "Beautiful," she said.

He seemed now to me—had always seemed—a pile of soiled feathers. "Peter? Beautiful?"

"That death," she said.

I knelt and touched the ear myself—the rules allowed that, now he was dead—brushed her own still finger, thought of a ship on the black Atlantic, in its white heart my love borne smiling away from me kneeling here, my throat crammed with knowledge that now was the time, that the time was past, to murder that love but powerless to serve myself, unkind.

SCARS

Sapped by a bath, Charles Tamplin slept on his back entirely naked but alone, unthreatened, leaned on only by afternoon sun, the light a quiet unneedful companion—as was the room. He had propped the room slowly round himself in the weeks since his first love failed and left; and though it was forming like a reef, with no plan, it seemed already (sparse as it was, awaiting funds) a sufficient fort against all but death. And portable—nothing his car couldn't haul wherever his future, his new self-sufficient life, would steer. "Companion and guard," he meant it to be; and the chief guards mounted watch now on his sleep—his books in shelves; on the desk a draft of half his thesis and notes for his novel; beside them a six-inch Japanese ivory (two men, a lady and a baboon dancing, tight in a ring, calligraphy all down the baboon's kimono); above on the wall two large dark etchings, one a perfect old German Rembrandt fake, the Hundred Guilder print, Christ ganged about by most of His life (disciples, Pharisees, the sick in carts, children for blessing); the other, genuine (bought with the savings of his recent solitude), Picasso's naked minotaur by a sleeping woman, his huge left arm lifting her cover, right arm extended—extending?—toward her, both urgent and static; she naked and plain, bleached in moonlight, oblivious but troubled.

His own sleep—a nap before cold supper, work—was as soothed and restorative as a child's, neither hectic nor drowned. His dream told him that—hardly a dream, a simple sense of walking alone, of seeing through clear eyes an entire world less free than himself, hostages given by all but him.

Yet the moment a hand touched the door of his room, turned the knob to enter, he leapt the two long steps to the opening door and reached for his wet towel hung on the knob. A strong woman's hand had reached round before him and, gripping the towel, pulled it slowly outwards into the hall. He said "No!", seized an end and tugged toward himself. The other hand fought for a moment, viciously; then slackened, yielded but not before the door was open on his instant of nakedness, two women's staring grins. In his panic they both seemed strangers, threats.

But when he was covered, the near woman moved in on him, still laughing, said, "Laid out for love, eh? Then why so shy?" His landlady Bett. But the other was strange, no one he had seen though she laughed like his oldest acquaintance, shared his secrets. When he backed away from Bett, the stranger followed to the center of his room—larger than Bett, younger (maybe forty), handsome, almost grand like a high leather chair, ample, tawny, all surface, hard. Bett spoke first—"We're going to the laundry. Give us your towel." She poked his ribs. No word of who the stranger was though he watched only her, her knowing eyes.

Bett had moved behind him so he spoke backwards to her. "I'm using it. You startled me. Step outside and you're welcome to it. I was sleeping. You startled me."

The stranger said, "—Frightened you. You're pale all over."

Bett said, "You seen more of him than me then. Let's have a look." She lunged from behind to strip off his towel.

He laughed for the first time, twisted his shoulders to throw her off and held the towel round him with two clenched hands, easily winning.

But the stranger rushed on him when their gaze had broken and, with only her hands, pressed his wrists to his sides—her hands inhuman, a hot machine.

At once his mouth was brassy with fear; and in one convulsion he threw Bett backwards, freed a hand, hit the stranger hard across the mouth—he felt the silent wet of her inner lips, her brittle teeth.

Bett stayed giggling where he'd flung her—by his cupboard.

The strange woman stood, one hand across her mouth, concealing his stroke, eyes smiling no longer, tight with rage. Then her hand dropped and he saw from her mouth jagging down to her chin a purplish scar, old but burning—as though he had struck her days ago and she'd stood here badly healing in his presence.

The time that followed had the quality of time (pressure, weight)—three seconds, maybe four, in which he was locked with this woman he'd offended, the last two alive, only two ever alive and eternal; he brute, she victim. Time and a sudden silent act which were both his familiar home and his prison. He saw of course his mother's face, Sara his love's, in the stranger's, half-hidden but judging, waiting, two feet away.

They were rescued, freed, by a ripe banana which Bett extended across his shoulder, saying loudly and laughing, "Here Mary, take this home to Ron."

The woman looked toward the banana, took it, laughed to Bett—"Right!"—weighed it plump on her palm, dandled it three times, then looked back to him —"May I have it please?"

He could not hear at first, still held by her scar— his scar for a moment, made and borne by him—so Bett moved beside him, poked him again. "Let her have it. Sure. Cost you—what?—all of four pence. Her need is greater than thine by far."

Mary studied it again as though it mattered. "I don't think I've had one since oh before the war. Never got back in the habit of buying them."

Bett said, "Don't give us that. You had them all during the war. I *know*. Lovely young chaps, dances every night—"

Mary asked him again, "May I have it please?"

"Mary *who?*" he said. "We haven't met."

"Blimey O'Reilly!—old Mary," Bett said. "Mr. Tamplin, *you* know. You've heard me recounting her escapades half the mornings you're here, remember?"

He remembered and smiled. "My name's Charles Tamplin."

Mary said, "I know. Know lots about you."

"Oh?" he said and pointed to the fruit (intended for his supper), "Yes, take it. Gladly. Glad to be of service." He grinned—"Put it to good use, I trust."

"None better," Bett said. "No needier cause. Her poor Ron's a candle in August, ain't he, Mar—"

"Hush," Mary said. "I make do, don't I?"

He saw she had said it to him—not leering—but

he had no answer, joking or serious; indeed, felt nothing but a mild unease at their being here at all in the
midst of his nap, he stranded in a towel.

Bett answered. "You make do, all right. Watch
you don't do somebody in—somebody like yourself."

Mary said—still to him, "I watch. I watch. You
believe, I watch. But I take every chance too. Know
every path, above-ground and under. I'm *having* my
life."

"Have on," Bett said, "but have it on your own
time please, not mine. I'm washing clothes before
Buck's tea—that's flat." She passed them both and
stood in the door. "Come on, Mary, get yourself out so
old Modesty can hand us his fig-leaf."

"I'm noticing his things," Mary said and moved
deeper inward, stood against his desk, her broad thighs
pressed hard into the edge. She quickly looked at the
etchings above. Then she looked down and touched his
straight rows of work and plans, lightly with her one
free hand—manuscripts, note-books, ink-bottles, pens
—as though she were blind and they each might be one
word of a message, or as though she had grace and were
blessing them. She looked back to him—"How on
earth do you do it?"

He noticed for the first time her pleasing voice—
calm, without Bett's highs-and-lows and one firm rung
up the accent-ladder from Bett's proud harshness. "Do
what?" he said, uneasier still.

"Sit here day in, day out; do your work?"

"Oh because I *know* my work," he said. "Know
the life I want and am going for it, here." He pointed
to the desk.

So she looked down again and saw his small ivory.

"Can I touch it?" she said.

"If you're careful," he said.

"Care's my middle name."

"—Like Hell," Bett said from a distance, collecting more wash from the bath, a room away.

But she already held it, with both hands gently, having laid the absurd banana down. "Is it real?" she said.

"*Real?*" he said—as though the lady, men and baboon moved in her hands and perpetually, in their smiling ring. What answer did she want? What answer did he need to give?

She meant the simplest. "Is it all handmade, I mean?"

"Oh yes," he said. "It's ivory. Carved two, maybe three, centuries ago."

"What's it say?" she said. She was stroking the text on the baboon's robe.

"Wish I knew," he said. "I showed it to a Japanese friend at college but he couldn't decide. It's an ancient script. I'll have to find a scholar. I think it's a poem—hope so, at least."

"I'll tell you," she said.

He smiled. "You know ancient Japanese?"

"No," she said, "but I know what all this means"—she held out the dancers, still carefully grasped, and waved her other hand back to the pictures. "Shall I make it a poem? I was good at poems, as a girl, in school."

"Yes," he said, sensing dread like a stir in the still, cooling air.

She studied it a moment, glanced again at the pictures, shut her eyes, creased her forehead, raised her

chin, lips apart—all the standard signs of creation.
Then she lowered her face, eye-level to him, looked at
him, moved her lips silently at first, then said "Hold-
Me-Not . . ." and stood another long moment silently,
lips moving still.

"That's your poem?" he said.

"Maybe not," she said. "Does it seem like a poem
to you? It's what came to me. A motto then. Say it's
my motto."

"Mine too," he said.

"I know," she said.

"Know what?"

"Know it's yours. Look at this—" She shook the
dancers precariously, waved back at the pictures—"And
you, standing there. No one's touching anyone in any
of this. Hands off. No holding." She had started the
sentence calmly, smiling; but the last four words
seemed said by her scar—he watched it redden, move
like a louder stronger mouth.

He shuddered once, passed it off as a shiver by
hugging his shoulders.

"You're cold," she said. "Here I'm growling on
and you're catching your death"; and again from the
bottom of the stairs, Bett called. Mary set the ivory in
its exact place, tapped the banana (now browning and
fragrant), said, "Thanks for the offer, Mr. Tamplin—
you're a gentleman—but I'll take my chances in the
cruel world." She laughed once and quickly moved past
him to the door, meaning to say nothing else, it
seemed.

But he ducked a little bow, still hugging himself,
and said to detain her, "The next time you come, I'll
be better dressed."

"You're dressed," she said—he flushed. "I've not even *seen* you, you're dressed so thick. Well, my hat's off to you, sweet love—good luck!" Before the heat eased in his head, she was gone, down the stairs, out the door, Bett mumbling behind her.

After all, they had left him his chilling towel. He unwound it, spread it on the ledge to dry and dressed for work, no further thought or hope of sleep. But when he was ready and went to the desk, the light from the window was too dim now; so he switched on his lamp, which lit the pictures he had meant to ignore (since Mary's poem), made the dancers gleam, warm though hard. He surrendered to her lethal discovery, fed on his treasures, now related and bared—no one touched in any of them. The dancers brushed one another's robes but no flesh met; only the baboon touched himself. The minotaur's arm withheld its intent (Picasso had said of it to Françoise Gillot, "It's hard to say what he wants—kill her or wake her"). And Rembrandt's Christ—he tried for the first time to count the figures: forty-five people (counting hats of the concealed), a camel, ass and dog, all in say sixteen-inches-by-eleven. Not one of them touched. Christ's hand extended toward a baby, two cripples' toward Him, a boy's toward his mother but none succeeded. Not one. Even mothers holding babies were touching only *cloth*. Space prevailed. Miracle, blessing, forever delayed though they waited in dusk—no light but His —and must always wait.

Early next morning at his table for breakfast, Charles Tamplin asked Bett as she huffed in with food (eggs, bacon, bread marooned in grease), "How old is your Mary?"

"How come?" she said; then stood before him, serious in her cooking smock—"Get your mind off Mary right now, Mr. Tamplin. She's in dirty trouble. In a mess, she is."

"My mind isn't on her. I only asked her age."

"I don't know that," she said. "Younger than me. But a damned sight too old to be mucking about with young chaps, I know."

He continued chewing through his own mild defense—"Oh she didn't bother me. I can take a joke. I was only startled, still half-asleep."

"Not you, fool," Bett said. "I know you're safe— Christ, padlocked and all now, ain't you? How's it feel?"

"Fine, Bett; feels fine—free air again." She was dusting now with the hem of her smock. "Then *who?*" he said.

"Mind your own business," she said, still dusting.

"Bett, you were the one shoved her into my bedroom on me, strip-naked. I don't send out engraved invitations to my afternoon naps. Not any more."

Bett did not beg pardon—the house was hers. She worked on awhile, plumping pillows, moving chairs (he had made his own bed); then began to talk on the move, as to herself—and from the beginning, her accustomed start. "The war must've done it. No, long before then she was wild as a cat. She grew up down the road from my Mum's. Being older, I'd left; was already married, but naturally I heard it all, *saw* a good slab of it when Mary went after Bill my youngest brother. But Bill had her beat from the start, he did—had more girls tucked away waiting on him than Samson had hairs. Which reminds me of the end of their la-de-da." Bett stopped and laughed. "Bill had give her the jilt one Saturday night, took some other girl to the dance, I reckon; and Mary dressed herself up and went down on the bus and walked in on them. She didn't raise Hell then-and-there for a change—found chaps to dance with and danced all night—but next morning, first post, Bill had a letter from her, careful, in ink. It said, 'Mr. Barnes, you have broke my heart and soon as my lovely new perm wears out, I'm drowning myself in the barge canal!' "

Bett stopped and acknowledged Charles Tamplin's presence—"Do you get her meaning, about her new perm? She meant *Piss off!* but she did say it clever, I'll grant her that. And she kept up a laugh through another year or so of slouching about. Her job (at a butcher's) was all that kept her from being a proper tramp—her time was limited. Her job and her Dad. Her Dad's all she ever loved, to this very day, for all her mess. And he caused half of it. He raised her, you see; let her have her way from the time she was twelve, when her mother died; just laughed when she told him her escapades though he's never known a tenth of the Hell she raised; and now he's old and can barely see, she don't even have to bother to lie. Still, she's good to him; pets him like a china doll—his heart's bad too. I've always said to Buck when he talked Mary down, told me not to see her, 'Buck, she's good as gold to her Dad.' '*Dad,* Hell,' Buck says. 'She's married to Ron and she treats Ron like dirt!' Buck's right and all. She always did. Ron's eat pecks of her dirt right from the start. Her teasing him on unmercifully, in her spare

time from others, till she had him worshiping, buying
her things arse-over-tip with every farthing from his
scrap of a job—lovely sweaters, fur-lined boots, things
to protect her (she'd rush stark-naked, arms open, into
a storm if its name was Fun). He was older than her by
five or six years, so he should have known better; but
somehow he got her in the family way—she *said* it was
Ron. Why I'll never know, if she hated his sight like
she says she does, unless it *was* his baby or unless the
other chaps involved had ducked out. Anyhow of all
things, she told her Dad; and he went to Ron, blue-
faced with rage, to say Ron must marry her. *Must!*
He'd have married her smiling if she'd been stuffed full
of a dozen babies, black as pitch.

"Well, married they were and the baby came—a
girl, nothing special. But Ron worshiped her too and
Mary settled in a bit and minded her duties. That's
when I made pals with her. Her and Ron and the baby
lived just down there then, near us; and me knowing
her since she was a girl, she came up most afternoons
for a chin-wag. I took to her right from the start. Buck
hated her. But I like a laugh—Christ, I've had a few—
and she'd come and put the baby in the corner to sleep
and then tell me all of her past escapades—what
lengths chaps had gone to even touch her wrist; how
she'd drive them up the wall night after night; then,
quick, give them a chance and they'd pop like crackers,
half-weep with joy! She kept me in laughs for months;
I'm still grateful. I'd always shove her off before Buck
was home. He could smell if she'd been there but he's
never run *me*. Then the baby died before anyone had
really noticed it—anyone but Ron, as I said. He was
crushed. Oh I don't mean to say Mary laughed at the

funeral. Of course she didn't. Her feelings are keen as a blade to this day—I'd no more mention that child to her than I'd spit in her face. But she healed, don't you know—quick, her old self again.

"The war had just started—I guess that was it— and everything was soldiers everywhere. Not Yanks— the Yanks didn't come for years, dirty dogs they was when they got here too—but good English boys, young as pups and scared stiff. Everything was 'doing your bit for the troops'; and as I've never knitted so much as a cap, I did my bit going to dances. Dances every night at the Assembly Rooms. Buck went along at first to help with the food (his shocking hernia kept him out)— keep an eye on me was his main intent. *I* was safe though, young as I was—oh I love to tease a sweet young chap; I'd get them so het-up they'd glow like grates but teasing was all. I'd dance like a dervish till five-to-eleven, then I'd dash for the last bus. Often I was chased but never caught! So Buck stopped going and I don't know who brought it up, me or her; but Mary went with me every night from then on—nights when I didn't go; dancing's not my *life*; I've had cares to attend to since I was a girl.

"When her and me went, she always came home with me. We'd get off the bus and there would be Ron, waiting to walk her home, the streets being black as pitch of course, blackout and all. It seemed to set her teeth on edge—Ron waiting. She'd give him a look like an open grave, then stump along home without a word, barely "Goodnight" to me. It got worse and worse—her resenting him there till one night she told him off with me looking on, words to make even me shiver, and I tried to leave; but she said, 'Wait, Bett, wait. Let's *all* wait here at the public bus-stop till James Ronald Campbell stiffens into a man.' Then she went up to him—it was a warm night, September, bright moon; he hadn't a coat on, only his jacket—and began pawing at him, stroking him up, saying, 'Now then, Cock, the Army won't have you. Let's see if *I* will. Let's see if you pass my test, old Cock.' He stood there and bore it too—as long as I watched. I broke away soon—and didn't seek her company for weeks after that. We met at the dances and she'd sit by me on the bus coming home; but she knew I was still sick from watching her show and she laid low awhile, where I was concerned —with Ron, too, it seemed. He had given up meeting her at the bus, and she never mentioned him no more than dust. *I* certainly didn't. He had my pity but not my respect—not after that night; for a while anyhow. I'd have knocked her flat—Buck would've killed me, soft-hearted as he is. What I couldn't understand was why he *stayed*—or let her stay, for she got far worse.

"Ron went on a night shift at the Works; and Mary started bringing chaps home, that's all. One night when I was still cool towards her, she climbed on the bus with this soldier, younger than her—she's always picked youth, except old Ron—and ginger-haired. Well, she set him by me on the long seat, you know, and made introductions polite as a party. You know I'm not nosey—I've got my own life to lead, which takes my time—but I reckon I all but amputated my tongue with my teeth on that ride. I nodded to her not him, and sat still. I was cold as marble and when the bus stopped I said to Mary, 'After you. Very far after you.' She said 'Righto!' and smiled and stepped off, her chap in hand. We went that way for weeks after too—

Mary in front with some new soldier (seldom one twice) and me behind. A time or two she tried to speak, turn and ask me questions—how was Buck and the dog? I'd ask her how was Ron and she'd say something cheeky—'Keeping busy' or 'Away a good bit'— but she stopped soon enough. She'd stopped coming round from the first awful night, and God knows I didn't set foot in their door. I didn't know what I might walk in on—some chap in his pants or old Ron hacking Mary down with a knife. The awful part is, I don't think he knew. I'd see the chaps leave her gate about dawn—she took *that* care—and Ron might have gone on in the dark till this day but that one night they had a power failure at the Works and Ron got home long before the dance ended.

"It was dead-winter, cold and pouring with rain; and when Ron come in, he must have found her boots in the hall. She'd left them; the rain hadn't started till late so he took it in his head to meet her at the bus and have her boots ready for her so she wouldn't spoil her shoes no worse than they were. The first sad thing was, the bus was late—maybe five or ten minutes—and Ron himself was soaked to the skin, just standing in the open, no shelter or nothing. I had stepped onto the platform early, ahead of Mary and this night's chap— I'd had enough of tailing her, like spying from behind —so I saw Ron first as the bus rolled past him; he had a little torch which of course was illegal. Christ, what could I do? Well, nothing. No time to gather my wits —and none of my business. I stepped down and shunned him—he didn't see me, wasn't *looking* for me. I tried to walk on but I had to look. I went a few yards, then turned and saw it by his dim little light. She leapt

off the bus nimble as a cat, the chap on her heels—not
so young this one and big, far bigger than Ron. She
took a few strides—head down in the rain, her chap a
bit behind—before she saw Ron. She stopped of course
but she never lost breath—why fear him *now*, was her
thought, I guess—and she said, 'What the Hell are you
up to, moping in the rain?' I could see him side-face.
He saw the soldier. Then he took a step to Mary. He
held out her boots and he tried to explain. He really
did. But he flung them in her face. He had bought
them; he figured they were his to use. They were good
boots, peace-time, fur-lined with brass buckles. One of
the buckles cut into her mouth. Which was when I left
—the sight of Mary all blood from the mouth down,
her soldier standing there dumfounded in the rain, old
Ron's mouth working still trying to explain. Well, I
left them to it—not from fear, understand; more like
disgust. My life is too short to stand by watching others
ruin theirs; I've got my *own* fight. And to this very day
I'm in total darkness about what happened after that
—who went with who, what awful things were said. I
didn't lay an eye on Mary or Ron for weeks after that,
more like months. For all I knew they were dead,
murdered, hanged. Well, they weren't. They had
moved. To Mary's father's. He had had a fall shortly
after that night, was crippled-up bad; so they moved in
with him, and there they've been ever since—what?
fifteen years."

"That's her scar," Charles Tamplin said. It was
not a question. He had finished his breakfast and, with
his right hand, traced the exact path of Mary's scar
down his face.

Bett said, "You noticed that. Don't miss a trick,

do you? Well, to be fair with you, I couldn't swear to
it. I didn't have her face memorized, you know; and
after that night it was so many months till I saw her
again that I didn't notice it right off. Buck did, at once.
We met her in a shop in town one morning—just
greeted one another—and the moment she left, Buck
said, 'Well, she got it.' '—Got what?' I said. '—What
she's been begging for. Someone knocked Hell out of
her mouth.' And I hadn't said a word to Buck about the
boots. Then I remembered—she'd held up her hand
when she spoke to us, like someone with new teeth,
shielding her mouth; but there had been a scar. So I
guess it was Ron. He'd marked her at last. And from
what I knew in years after that, Buck was right again—
the Hell *had* been knocked right out of her. Not that
she sprouted wings of course; but between her sick Dad
and whatever Ron had done, she kept home at night
for the rest of the war—long after the war. I say 'kept
home.' What I mean is, I didn't see her down at the
Assembly Rooms for years; and if she'd been dancing
between here and London, old Bett would have seen
her—*I* didn't stop but then I'd kept my head and all,
hadn't I?"

"Yes," Charles Tamplin said.

"Like you," Bett said.

He said "Thank you," smiled quickly—"But you
see her now. She's your friend again."

Bett said, "Never. Not my friend. I don't have
friends—no, I really don't. I've never felt the need. I've
had Buck of course all these years and Peter while he
lived and my old Mum; but the rest are just faces I
natter with, wave to as I go about my own business.
Mary, least of all—"

"But you see Mary. What about yesterday?"

"That's only her. The past few years she's begun dropping in. I give her a laugh—a little time-off from her old Dad and Ron. But it's got to stop—I must make it stop. She's dangerous, she is. Oh not to me—and not to you either; I was only joking a minute ago. It's herself she'll ruin of course—again. Herself and her poor Dad and Ron, though if you ask me, they'd be damned lucky if she took her lad and flew off to China."

"What lad?" he said.

"Don't ask me that. I know—know his name and his job (a chauffeur); but not *him*, thank God—and I'm sorry I know. She told me before I could stop her, bragged it to me—how he's put new life in her. If that's life, Christ! Deliver me. 'Life and hope,' she said. Hope for what?—a slit throat. He's a bad one, he is—this new one she's got. He'll throw knives not boots, you mark my words."

Bett had finished, he knew. That was often her exit—"Mark my words," a justified sibyl, generally right. She scratched at her hair, glanced toward his clock—"Crumbs! Half-past nine, and all *my* work! You can make me talk worse than anyone—and what about? Pure rubbish, I reckon. Your mind's meant to be on higher things. I thought that was your latest plan anyhow." She was sweeping his dishes onto a tray.

He did not answer.

"Eh?" she said and laughed and pointed to Picasso's naked woman, asleep while love or death poised above her—"Higher things such as that lady's bare bum, eh? You don't fool me."

"I *do*," he said. "I've fooled you completely" and

moved to his desk. But he said it to the walls. Bett was gone; hurled into her day, he thought, her desperate useless day.

And surely he had, for he spent the whole morning in his quiet room in the silent house and, ignoring lunch, on into the afternoon, not moving from his desk —beneath the lady's bum, Christ's hand (untouched, untouching), beside the dancers—writing into his notes, with sustained exhilaration of loathing, Bett's ragged wasteful gamy tale in Bett's own words of Mary entirely surrendered; and with—toward the end, as time reached the present, this warm afternoon—the thrill of power, to have gripped in his own hands this proper mess, this shoal of rubbish, and made it part of his own hard understanding of what, in the world, he could stride across; his own needs harnessed, tense but obedient. Then he read through the pages and wrote at the bottom these questions they raised—

—*The name of the story?* —Scars *perhaps.*
—*Why should Bett tell this story at all? Why is she so clearly fascinated by Mary that she tolerates her here against Buck's orders, after all this past and whatever is present and threatens now? Why tell it to me? Who am I—must she think—to need this news? (I am all she has—her Wedding Guest. She cannot speak of it to Buck or her mother, cannot even mention the past to Mary.)*
—*What is Mary's demon? Simple sexual famine? "Appreciation"? What is her vision of the life she insisted to me she was having? What has Ron withheld all these years—or lacked? Why—as Bett asks—has he not thrown her out or at least struck (or scarred) again?*

*Why—knowing what he knew—did he follow Mary to
her father's house?*
*—And who is her father in all of this? What does he
know of her? need from her? fear? Why is he her one
apparent pole?*
*—Why should she be anyone's pole, center?—least of
all, three mens': her old Dad's, Ron's, her lethal lad's?*
—Surrendered to what?

Then he clamped the pages neatly into his folder
—the latest in all that awaited him there, his past and
others', subdued but unfinished, requiring him. Then
he was tired—as exhausted as from love—so again he
lay on his bed, clothed fully, leaned on only by yellow
light, alone in the house.

He had slept an hour when the doorbell woke him
gently (a bell that worked on a wind-up spring always
unwound so that callers announced themselves timidly,
like broken toys). He lay a moment waiting for Bett's
footsteps—silence—so he stepped to his window and,
hid by the curtain, looked to the street. A clean black
Austin stood at the curb and a driver waited—or sat,
staring forward, not noticing the house: a man maybe
twenty, large head, black hair, hunched shoulders in
black, huge hands on the wheel. Was it he who rang?
No—the bell gave a final spent wheeze, a hand rapped.
He did not want to go and did not know why till a
voice called "Bett?"—Mary's voice, out of sight. He
would not go, had not made a sound, crouched in on
himself behind the curtain, then crept to his bed, lay
silently down and waited for Mary's footsteps depart-

ing. But the sound was the unlocked front door opening, Mary entering. Once more "Bett?", then "Mr.
Tamplin?", then her steps climbing quickly toward his
door.

He flung himself backward into feigned dead-sleep
so deep that when she knocked at last, he heard as in
paralyzed terror of dream, could not reply. But she
knocked again, then opened his door. He did not look,
lay still on his back, eyes clamped, unflickering—so that
while he had known the voice as Mary's, he could not
see her face (see *any* face yet) nor chart her progress
across his floor as her steps moved slowly toward his
bed. Her steps?—was it she? Was it Mary at all? Why?
Come for what? And was his sleep sham? Was he
locked in actual nightmare now or was someone, something, here by his bed, above his vulnerable body,
poised unseen for an unknown purpose? He wished to
scream. Scream what?—*Help* or *Leave?* And scream to
whom? He saw faces now. The old faces rose as they
had yesterday and would always rise; each, judge and
victim. He fought them off, fought back a scream by
clenching his jaws again and again.

"You kept your promise." She spoke above him.

He opened slowly on Mary's face, her scar
smoothed off by the tension of a smile, her black coat
open, touching his bed. "What promise?" he said. He
remembered none.

"—To carry me away to America and happiness."

He was genuinely dazed from his sham sleep, his
terror. "When did I promise that?"

"You don't remember? *Shame,*" she said. "I suppose you promise that to every girl. You Yanks *are*
rotten." But her smile hung on.

"I'm sorry," he said. "My promises now are all to myself."

"No," she said. "Sweet love, don't fear. I'll survive somehow." Then she laughed (her scar returned)— "What a face! Don't weep. *I've* made arrangements. No, I meant you had promised to be better dressed when we met again."

He studied his body a moment, relieved. "So I am," he said. He smiled, sat up. "Bett's out, of course."

"Out where?" Mary said, suddenly efficient.

"Her mother's, I guess."

"When's she due back here?"

"God knows," he said. He stood, took the steps to reach his open door, took his post there to see her out.

"Where's Buck?" she said.

"At work, I'm sure. Bett's always home before Buck, making tea."

"Then we'll wait," she said.

"For what?"

"Not *us*, sweet love—not you and me. My friend in the car—" Mary pointed to the street. "We'll wait in Bett's sitting room. I'll call him in." She moved toward the door, one step from Charles Tamplin.

He shut the door, shut them both in his room. "Bett's is locked," he said, speaking rapidly. "She always locks their part of the house whenever she leaves. Got in the habit when the dog was alive—Peter being so ferocious, would push doors open and lunge after me if I made a sound. No it's locked, I know—"

Mary smiled again slowly. "Up here," she said. "There's rooms up here. The stairs aren't locked. No way to lock them. *I'm* here, look."

He thought a moment, leaned against his shut

door. "Buck," he said. "Buck may come any time. He's often early."

"Let him come," Mary said. Her smile was set now. "Let him join the party."

"I'm leaving too," he said. "I must run into town." His door stayed shut.

"Can we stay here then?" She gestured behind her, meaning his room.

He looked past her, followed her pointing hand. The room—walls, bed, desk, papers, pictures—seemed blotched and stinking as though her hand had blindly sown stain, as though he must scrape it all, scour it with acid before he could rest again, work again here. He faced her—"Please. No." It was begging—he the beggar.

"You know what I'm asking for?"

He nodded.

"Only this much space—" In the air she measured off the width of two bodies.

He nodded, shut his eyes.

"You know what I've been through in my so-called life?—Bett's told you of course—and you won't help me into this new chance I've found?"

He would have to look. He looked. She seemed young—taut with her hunger—but he shook his head, no.

"That's final?" she said.

He nodded, yes.

"Let me out," she said.

Then he saw that he blocked her, still leaned on his door. He opened it slowly, took a step aside; and she left through the narrow space, not touching him at all —no further word or look. But he shuddered in the chill air that moiled behind her; and though he heard the click of the gate, the black car leaving, old safety of silence, it heaved in his throat, slapped his teeth like nausea—suspicion that his room, his life in this house was ruined, fouled at least; infected by exposure to virulent dependence, the lethal illusion of contingency, the sight of lives propped together like cards, humped down like dominoes, a fallen row. Could a room recover, serve him again?

He stood in his open door facing downward—the yellow hall; unable to take one backward step or look. He touched his pockets—car keys, wallet. He could walk straight forward, door open, no message; abandon all this as tainted burden; go like Bunyan's Christian, stripped for the journey. Journey to where? He was three thousand miles from America his home. Cornwall perhaps?—Tintagel, grand shattered bone barnacled by tearooms. The Scilly Islands?—a bland Indies. Or Brighton?—the home of his nearest friend, acquaintance really, a fellow student now teaching there, sharing rooms with his mother high back on the chalk in sight of a sea flat as gray ditch water.

Nonsense. Weak nonsense. His work was his journey; work his home—in the midst of whatever. And thinking of Brighton, he recalled unfinished work, notes he must make on a recent trip there, a scene to store, both eye and shield. He turned, faced his room —already cleansed—walked quickly to his desk and began to write, from flawless memory—a title first, *Seeds*. Then

David Caldwell invited me to Brighton for Easter —two weeks in advance, by letter, promising sun. I had meant to refuse and work on here; but early one morn-

ing I dreamt his death, in the form of a story my
mother tells of her brother in France in the first World
War—how he and a boyhood friend from home sat
playing cards with others in a trench, took a direct hit
from a German shell, and how my uncle looked round
(in what light?), saw the others dead and his friend
prone beside him. But his friend's heart beat (he swore
that always), an artery pumped live blood from a
shoulder; so my uncle took him up, bore the friend in
his arms like a child—how far? Say a hundred yards to
a small aid station, told the man on duty (another
friend), "He's alive, work fast," then laid his friend
down and looked in full light. His friend lacked a head.
The blood that had pumped from the stump of his
neck was already drying. I dreamt that of David—I my
uncle, he my friend; the identical story except that I
bore David miles not yards through a no-man's land
white and rough as the moon—and woke so depressed
that I stumbled through the morning unable to work,
resisted the urge to phone and confirm he was still
alive. We are not close friends.

    But at noon I did write and accept his invitation,
still not wanting to go but curious now to crack my
dream. So on Friday I spent three maddening hours on
the Brighton road, reached the Caldwell's at five and
was met by the mother—David out with his girl. The
mother (Nell Caldwell) is fiftyish, small, steady on
thick legs. Beneath brown hair fine and thin as a
baby's, her round face smiles perpetually, from the nose
downward. Her eyes, cheeks, forehead are lined, gathered, never relaxed. Is she worried, fearful, on guard?—
against what? She has only one fear left—her own
death (or David's, I suppose, though they move so

separately of one another, more like bees in a hive—
considerate but busy—than mother and only child, that
I doubt his death would break her stride). She has
weathered all the rest—the death of her father when
she was eleven; the need then for her to stop school,
nurse three brothers; her early marriage in the deepest
Depression to a boy from Kent, named Jack, who sold
shoes and lived above the shop in two rooms where she
joined him, to wait out the worst of those years—they
hoped—before having a son, in '38. Then the war, the
raids—she was caught in London the first day of bomb-
ing, waited in the Tube beneath Victoria Station till
the trains recommenced, not knowing what ruins
Brighton might be in, nor Jack nor David—"They were
well," she says, "Jack had worried over me, when I'd
told him before, 'I'm a born hedgehog—duck under
danger'; but there I'd seen them in my mind all day at
the top of those stairs, David naked in the air, less than
two years old, just tiles between them and whatever
chose to fall. But they were well—Jack and David—
and laughing, I felt I could kill them after all my
worry."

Jack was dead in six months—called into the
Army, sent to train in Kent near his father's home and
killed when a lorry overturned on his cycle (he a motor-
cycle messenger). Nell had told me that much on two
previous visits, at times when David was out or sleeping
—she does not recall the past in his presence. Why?
But this day, this gray Good Friday, she finished the
tale—how she and a friend had taken young David by
bus to Worthing (a Sunday outing) and were sitting
there near the front with him—he was playing on some
public child's equipment, still open for use despite the

threats. "It was near tea-time," she told me, straight at
me. She never looks down, always holds to your eyes as
though they were straps but without that starved intensity of unhappy women. We were seated in the
parlor before a small fire—"and I'd said to Kay my
friend that we must go. David looked really frozen
though he still played on—even then, still not three, he
played like a Turk, hands white with pressure as he
seized iron bars on the swing or whatever. Kay looked
at her watch and said, 'A bus is just due'; so I ran for
David who began to cry at the sight of me; and odd as
it seems—though I knew he cried not to leave his game
—I said to myself in my head as I ran, 'Oh what does
he know? Why cry? Why cry?' Then Kay said, 'Don't
run. What luck! Look here.' I had not reached David
but I stopped and looked—he bawling louder, three
steps away. I did not go for him; for what Kay had seen
was Fred my brother in his scrap of a car, stopping by
Kay. Fred was younger than me but the Army wouldn't
have him—spotty lungs like our father. I took a few
steps on towards Fred, quite baffled—why on earth was
he here, mid-afternoon? I remember mostly feeling
anger—strange. So angry I forgot David crying behind
me. Perhaps he had stopped, gone back to play—yes,
he must have done. What I did was stand quite a
distance from Fred—still in his car—and call to him
harshly, 'You should be at work' (as though the little
work he could manage, at a stationer's, would hold off
Hitler, win the war). Then he came towards me—
passed Kay as silent as a cloud of smoke—and as
David had with me, I knew at once. Though I didn't
cry. To this day, I haven't cried—not for Jack." She
stopped and rose and poked the fire but not from

emotion; her eyes were dry—the fire was low, it needed attention; so she worked with it patiently.

Not wishing to speak, least of all to question, I looked to a table where a picture was propped in a yellow wood frame—*Jack*, I knew; she had told me before. I'd have known anyhow. The head, face, shoulders are an outline of David's, an exact silhouette. The face is older—not in actual years (it was made when Jack was about David's age, 22, 23) but in form, evolved form. It is still the face of a Kentish farmer, each feature rounded as by ages of water or scoured by ice. David's face is finer, newer, unworked, unworn —a memory of his father's but also a correction.

Perhaps she saw me looking and dreaded a question; so she said, "I'm afraid I must leave you now— shocking David, still gone! I must run to my mother's, warm her meal"—(her mother, past eighty, lives alone down the hill, refuses to leave though her mind is gone; sees herself in a mirror and tells Nell a woman is trapped behind glass, leaves plates of chilled food by the mirror to feed her)—"You'll read here, won't you? David's due any moment." I said "Of course" and then in the front door we heard a key turn—David finally. Yet we both stood and waited as though uncertain, for a total stranger, purpose undeclared.

Four unseen strides and he stood in the open door, facing us—David of course though he did not speak. He grinned to me but greeted his mother—in an odd slow bow, deep from the waist, made entirely for Nell, face unsmiling, extended right hand barely grazing the rug, left hand clenched at the small of his back; then slowly rising till he faced her solemnly and suddenly grinned, still to her, all for her. That was what puzzled me—*the degree of attention; why? was he tipsy?—but I laughed as he rose and, it being Good Friday, said, "Lo, he is risen—and two days early!"*

His mother's eyes brimmed tears, had surely produced them before my tasteless joke. Now we all stood baffled till Nell could speak (her tears never fell, drained back as quickly as they came)—"Tell me where you learned that?" —"Learned what?" David said. —"That bow for me . . ." He began it again—he was slightly high—"In my own sweet heart, I have made it for you," completed it poorly, then dashed for the toilet.

Nell turned to me, said with startling vehemence, "His father's bow, Jack's greeting to me after every parting. David never saw that, can't remember that, less than two years old when Jack last left." Then she asked me to judge—"Is it memory, you think?" I had not thought it out; but I said what she needed, "Memory, surely. It must be memory"; yet before she had cleared the doorsill, leaving, I said to myself, "It was surely a seed, buried in his conception, to flower now."

That was all, he thought—more poem than story, only the crushing metaphor of David's bow—and glancing back, he thought it was finished, solved, as his record of Bett's long tale was not. He knew no questions to ask of this—except, metaphor of what? and why the bow should have surfaced when it did, why not years before, years later, why to Nell? What could it tell her? What use could it be now but pain renewed? So, calmed, his sense of control firmer now, he stood and thought he would rest awhile—not sleep or escape but a short reward, a drive in the country, supper in Burford.

He was in his coat and down in the hall, when he saw, through the opaque front-door glass, a large close shape. He stood quiet, waited—Bett? Buck? surely not Mary again? The door was not locked but the dead bell rustled a half-turn, stopped. He checked his watch. It could not be Mary—too near Buck's tea-time—so he moved forward quickly and opened on a tall man, thin, mid-forties, cloth cap held in twitching hands.

The man's eyes hunted Charles Tamplin's face for a silent moment. Then he withdrew a step and studied the house-number screwed to the wall, looked backward to his bicycle propped by the gate. The right house, yes. His face tightened, filled from within as from pressure, fury, sudden youth; but his hands still twitched. "Betty?" he said.

Charles Tamplin said, "Bett? She's out, I'm sorry."

"Oh," the man said, turned his hat half round in his kneading hands, found his next request—"Will you give her a message? I'd be most grateful."

"I'm sorry, I'm just going out myself. You could leave a note."

The man nodded slowly and shut his eyes, stood in place but rocking.

Charles Tamplin turned inward. "I'll get some paper—"

The man gave a sound—a croak, a grunt.

Charles Tamplin looked. The man's face was white, tears poured down his cheeks, fell on his topcoat, his thin lips worked—open, shut, silently. Charles Tamplin stood where he was, in the hall, three steps from the man. "Are you all right?" he said.

The man shook his head but did not go. So they both stood like challengers, unthinking but adamant. Then the man found his voice—"Let me in for a moment please. Betty's a friend."

"Her rooms are locked." He pointed behind him as simple proof.

"I'll stand in the passage." The man pointed also —beggary, the second time today.

Charles Tamplin said "Yes" and, not wanting to open his own room now, searched in the drawer of the hall table. He found a used envelope, took his own pen and gave them to the man now standing inside.

The man said "Thank you," stubbed the corners of his eyes with a thumb and wrote his message slowly but fluently, well-prepared, bearing hard on the uncovered surface of the table as though permanently gouging whatever he must say.

Charles Tamplin waited till the man stood, finished, eyes red but drying. "If you leave it there, they'll see it, I'm sure." Then he buttoned the last few buttons of his coat to remind the man.

The man understood, squared the envelope neatly dead-center on the table, returned the pen. Half-turned to go, he caught his own face in the small dull mirror, shook his head at himself but without expression, neither smile nor frown. He went to the door, said to Charles Tamplin, pausing but not looking back, "I'm very grateful." Then he left.

When the shadow had faded beyond the glass, Charles Tamplin read the note—not lifting, not touching it; from two feet away, its round script as legible as epitaph—

Dear Betty and Buck:—Mary left a note sometime today to say she is gone for good at last. I do not know to where or who with if anyone but her Dad found the news before I was home and had a bad spell with his heart, worst yet. I found him half-dead on arrival from work. He is going to hospital now, by ambulance. It looks like the end. If you meet Mary anywhere, tell her this. She will want to know.

> *Many thanks,*
> *Ron Campbell*

His first clear thought was "Grateful for what?" Ron's final thanks flung shame in his face, for coldness, impatience, and worse—for waste, the wasted chance for answers to questions Bett's story had raised; Mary's life had raised, her father's dependence, Ron's vacant abandoned spectacle. Why had any sane man collapsed in the hole of Mary's departure?—small vacuum surely, welcome relief. But then he wondered "When did she go?" and his own neutrality was breached. Suppose that today, this afternoon, Mary's own intent had been no worse than to bring her man to Bett's, use him here somehow in Buck's certain absence (maybe only show him off) and that by Bett's absence and his own refusal to play the dingy game, he had fanned her fury, burnt her bridges for her, unknown to himself, sent her home to leave her final note. Suppose what else?—that she left her note, abandoned her life and came here to bend above his fake nap and joke with him? The hall was cooling though not yet cold; but Charles Tamplin shook against his will—a shudder at first as though rousing himself, then a long moment, violent (neck rigid, eyes shut, hands clenched beside him) as he faced his probable part in the day, his choice of amends.

No choice in fact; one distant chance—find Mary, take her to her father in time. Find Mary where? Her man had waited at the curb in a car. They could be forty miles away by now, on the edge of London, total escape. His only hope was Bett, that Bett knew more than she'd told and would help. Again he checked his watch. It was time for her here, Buck's tea-time shortly. But she often missed that if her mother was low, left Buck to himself and came much later.

He would go to her mother's on the far side of town, beyond the station. (He knew the house, had driven Bett there through snow one day—a row house, grimy stripe of brick.) He had reached the door before he thought of the note—the note was not his but if Buck came first, found the news before Bett, she would have Hell to pay, days of justifying; or Buck might destroy it, never tell Bett a word.

He stepped back, took the note, folded it once, held it in his right hand—no hint of concealment—and went out the door.

He drove slowly over Bett's usual route, searching each cyclist's exhausted face as he flanked it, passed. No sign of Bett. She still waited safely at her mother's, surely. He felt that, trusted that, as strongly as if Bett were a magnet concealed in the town, pulling him effortless, powerless to her, her battered simple self his urgent goal—rest, forgiveness, sanction for his course.

The road ahead—to the next long curve—was clear of riders now. Free for a moment and elated, he gained speed; but round the curve was the city coach station (a paved square packed with red and green buses). The stretch past that seemed a thicket to him. He slowed, threaded carefully through cyclists, children, old ladies on foot; then was stopped by a light, surrounded by a surge of homebound workers. His eyes flicked rapidly across each face—no Bett. Then the light went yellow. A final couple crossed, taking infinite time as though pavement were bog. The light was green but he could not move. They were passing his front bumper, looking ahead to a cranking coach—LONDON. Mary and her man, unsmiling in black coats, their hands entirely empty. They broke into a trot—the coach door was closing.

Charles Tamplin rammed through the intersection, stopped by the far curb and ran back loudly— the coach door was closed, smoke chuffed from the rear. He reached it midway along its length, struck the green side with both hands open. The motor calmed, door opened for him. But he stood where he was, looked up to the windows and saw Mary's face two feet above him, knowing but grave, locked behind thick glass, her man dim beyond. "Your father is ill," Charles Tamplin said.

She could not hear, pressed nearer the pane.

He spoke slowly, mouthing a visible message— "Your father's near death. His heart. Wants you."

She heard, nodded once—message delivered, then looked away, not to him or her lad but forward, the driver's neck, the road; her profile expectant, lifting, like a girl's.

The door shut and though Charles Tamplin struck again, the coach left him gagging in blue exhaust, encased in haze, a harmless ghost.

But he *saw*, with new clarity, Mary's gift—ten yards away his abandoned car, a tall policeman tagging it grimly (no waiting of course); in clots, the stalled white faces of passers, stopped by his scene (as outraged by noise as baffled by his purpose), intent on finding a way to ignore him, hopeful only that his little racket would not demand help, not keep them from home ten seconds longer, not change their lives.

He would not—he saw—maybe could not change another life, surely *had* not ever. He only, in the jostling world, safe alone; for he also saw that the name of all stories was Scars not Seeds—all stories but his. Scars made and sought, gladly begged, grinningly killingly *rightly* pursued—by Mary, her lad, weak Ron, her father; by Bett, Buck, David, Nell, Sara his own chance he'd stripped from himself, his uncle bearing a headless friend; by the minotaur, the woman (whether death or embrace), Christ's impatient hands yearning for nails, the dancers launched smiling into hot exhaustion. All surrendered but him. He envied them all. For this moment, he worshiped their wasteful courage, ruinous choices, contingency. The name of his story was, what? —Flight, surely. Would always be. His car was free now, policeman gone, faces dispersed. He took its roof as a still point, a guide, that might welcome him. Then he jogged toward it, speaking his love's name silently, lips gaping slowly with each hard step, a fish in air, a hostile element.

WAITING AT DACHAU

THE CAMP ITSELF—its active life—only lasted twelve years ('33–45). Twelve years after that, we parked by its gates. Now, twelve years after that, I still don't know; the question has gathered force with every year's distance—why did you balk and refuse to enter Dachau, letting me, forcing me to go in alone? I need to know several things—my version, your version, then the truth.

Is the answer simple?—you were sick or tired or fed-up with sights after six-weeks' traveling? Or were you miffed about the night before, or—being a little younger—you may not have seen my urgent need, as a radio-and-newsreel child of the Forties, to test my memories against the source? (Dachau and I are almost exact contemporaries; I'm one month older than it and still running.) For months in advance, I'd braced for the prospect. Me at the Abyss—*us*, don't you see?—the heart of darkness head-on, between the eyes. (What did I expect?—to stagger? vomit? No, I knew all wounds would be internal, all effects delayed.) Or maybe you understood quite well—you and your Imagination of Disaster—and were only invoking your famous policy of kindness-to-self. Surely, though, your chances of bearing-up were as good as mine—we'd been told the camp was hip-deep in flowers! Couldn't you have entered as a simple gift to me?

Well, you didn't. You waited. The last time you waited—for me, at least—and I still wonder why.

My version is this: we'd planned it from the first. Christmas vac. of my first Oxford winter you'd flown from Paris and we'd stretched on the frigid floor of my digs, maps and budgets around us, and plotted the summer (should it ever come: your nosedrops had frozen on my bureau Christmas Eve!)—a slowly warming arc. You would join me again in mid-July. We would ship my new Volkswagen—Newcastle to Bergen. Then we'd push slowly on—a week each for Oslo, Stockholm, Copenhagen; then a non-stop plunge through Germany to Munich. Dachau.

Why Dachau at all? We passed within twenty miles of Belsen, Nordhausen, Dora, Buchenwald, Ohrdruf, Flossenburg. Dachau was never a major death camp. Only a third of its inmates died. Yet I never considered another camp. Three reasons, I think: I knew it was there (most others were razed); the name itself was the perfect emblem, as it was for the Germans themselves, it seems—anyone who disappeared was assumed "to be in *Dachau*." (Something inheres in the name, the sound—pronounced correctly it contains an unstopped *howl*. So does *Auschwitz* but Auschwitz could be—for Americans born after 1950—a brand of beer; *Buchenwald* could be a national park; *Belsen* a chocolate factory. *Dachau* seemed to me then—and seems now—only a terminus; last-stop, as Auden knew in '38—

> . . . *the map can point to places*
> *Which are really evil now—*
> *Nanking. Dachau.*)

And then nearby was Salzburg, as antidote—*Figaro* with Schwarzkopf, Fischer-Dieskau, Seefried, Karl Böhm. Then we could slowly climb the Rhine to Cologne (still without a whole building), the Hague and Vermeer, Amsterdam and Rembrandt; then (healed by now, stronger for the burns), we would ship back to Oxford, take a look at our gains, our chances, maybe marry. You'd pack up your chaste tight paintings in Paris (adjectives yours—triangles, oblate spheroids, cubes, all aching with loneliness in empty space) and join me for a last Oxford year on my thesis; then we'd sail home to all the books I'd write (my dreams of extracting love from my past, the boneyard of my childhood)—having already, well before we were thirty, faced the worst that life had ever offered any human pair, the final solution.

We made it to Munich precisely on schedule, only slightly in the red and apparently in love after four weeks of cold-water hosteling, cold roadside meals— canned potato salad, canned corned beef; we had bought a case of each and would only need bread every day at noon. I keep a photograph of one of those lunches—even without it, I'd have it in my head. We have stopped for lunch by a lake somewhere between Geilo and Oslo. Clear sky, the light a lemon yellow. You sit on a large stone, ten yards from the water, surrounded by smaller stones round and large as baseballs. The sounds are: our feet in those stones, water stroking, your opening of cans. I squat watching you warmed to fragrance in the light, adding to my luck

only one more sound—in my head, the voice of Flag-
stad. She is still alive, a hundred-odd miles from here in
retirement, playing solitaire and knitting—and that
voice like a new lion in a zoo, *intact!* If she'd sing now
we'd hear it cross valleys, through pines! (she will of
course return to make those last recordings which
calmly eliminate all future need for Wagnerian so-
pranos). You speak—"Sir, your lunch." You are holding out your hand with a plate of food but you have
not risen. I must come to you. Halfway is halfway. I
rise and go. *The happiest day in all my life*—I say that
silently, moving toward you. Now, twelve years later, it
is still unassailed. There hasn't been a happier. Yet,
how do I have this photograph of it, in which your
hand and the plate of food are blurred, moving toward
me? Did I force you to offer it again for the camera or
had I waited, shutter cocked, for the moment? Why
did you let me complicate your simple service?—you
smile in the picture but you have at least the grace to
refuse to meet my eyes. Your refusal has begun; your
heels are digging in. I am drowned, though, in what
tastes to me like good fortune; so I fail to notice for
weeks, days or nights.

In the days I could see you—walking gravely past
acres of Norwegian painting (every painting since the
war in shades of pink and yellow) to smile and say at
last "A nation of fairies!" Or sitting in a Stockholm
park, eavesdropping on a Swedish girl and her compact
rapidly heating French boyfriend (the girl so liberated
that I all but expected a taut diaphragm to pop out and
roll to rest at our feet when she uncrossed her legs),
you said, "Knock her up and she'll wail like Queen
Victoria!" Or stopping in the midst of tons of bland

Thorwaldsen marbles in Copenhagen (all like variations on the head of Mendelssohn)—"Well, I like the
Danes. They're crooks." Setting those down makes you
sound studied, tough; a big reader of Salinger and Mary
McCarthy. But I *saw* you. You were then, every minute
of those long summer days, the perfect customized
answer to all my optical needs. You seemed—you
threatened!—to lack outer boundaries, integument; to
vibrate within only vaguely held limits which, each
night, permitted—welcomed!—me in to form a perfect
compound.

Was I wrong, self-deceived, about that as well? I
could even see you then—by the Midnight Sun; the
birds never slept. Were you merely drumming time
through all my happy hours of artful plunging? (the
years spent studying van de Velde, Eustace Chesser)?
It's accurate, I know, to say you never turned to *me*. I
was the one to initiate action. But once I had laid a
hand on your hip, you would rock over toward me and
open like—gates! Very earnest, weighty gates that not
every man could move. And you'd smile and *thank me!*
Always at the end—and you almost always made it or
threw Oscar-winning acts—you would say (not whisper; have you still never whispered a word in your life?)
"Thank you" as though I had zipped the back of your
dress or made you a small expensive gift (when there
stood my donor capped with high-smelling rubber, Res-
ervoir Tipped to *block* small expensive gifts). And
that in the Fifties before the Revolution, when ninety-
eight percent of the girls I'd had still shuddered at the
end and asked forgiveness—asked me, Count Vronsky!
I would lie some nights for hours, too grateful to sleep.
You'd be gone in ten seconds.

Was I really wrong? Wasn't the only bad night the one in Munich? Where did we sleep there?—some station hotel or with one of our specialty, war widows with lace-curtained bedrooms to rent and permanent frozen killing smiles propped round government-issue teeth? I can't see the room but I heard the silence— that I took you, really *had* you, against your will for the first time ever. You were tireder than I; but even then you laughed when I'd hacked to my reward, all huffs and puffs, and questioned your stillness. You said— *said!* surely our *Witwe* heard you—"Riding shotgun in a Volkswagen daily leaves a body badly tuckered." Well, pardon me, Sara—twelve years too late, if you even remember. Hadn't all the other sex till then though been mutual? Wasn't it *love?* We had known each other for ten years exactly, grown up together. We knew all the ways—more than half of them hidden —to protect each other; and any damage was a slip, inadvertent. We could have lived together as easily as dogs; and I'd thought—till that day at Dachau—we meant to. If we didn't love each other, who ever has?

    —The de Wieks anyhow, if nobody else. You won't have heard of them. I hadn't till two years after we parted—in Ernst Schnabel's book on Anne Frank. A Dutch Jewish husband and wife flushed from hiding in 1943 and shipped to Auschwitz, where the husband died and the wife survived to remember Anne Frank's death. But this is the thing I want you to know—Mrs. de Wiek's memory fifteen years later of a moment on the packed train threading toward Auschwitz:

> *I sat beside my husband on a small box.*
> *The box swayed every time the wheels jolted*

*against the tracks. When the third day came
and we had not arrived, my husband took my
hand and suddenly said: "I want to thank
you for the wonderful life we have had together."*

*I snatched my hand away from him,
crying: "What are you thinking of? It's not
over!"*

*But he calmly reached for my hand
again, and took it, and repeated several times:
"I thank you. Thank you for the life we have
had."*

*Then I left my hand in his and did not
try to draw it away . . .*

There is no photograph in the book of him or her;
but they've walked, since I read that, as clearly in my
head, as in *Daniel* three just Jews walk safe through the
flames of Nebuchadnezzar's furnace. Shadrach, Me-
shach, Abednego—and a fourth, their angel. The de
Wieks walk alone, two stripped Dutch Jews, dark-eyed,
grinning, safe in my head; to Hell with *my* head, safe
through all time should *no* one know of them, sealed in
the only knowledge that turns fire—to have loved one
another through to the last available instant, to have
known and then had the grace to say thanks.

Were you just not that good—that strong and
pure—or did you choose not to be that good *for me?*

I see them in their flames (or you by your lake)
much more clearly than I see Dachau. My world-
famous total recall deserts me. Or does it? Can it have

been the way I remember? (I've never gone again.) The latest *Britannica* gives this much—that Dachau is a town eleven miles northwest of Munich, population ('61) 29,086, first mentioned as a market village 805 AD and continued as a village till 1917 when an ammunition factory was built there—the site in March 1933 of the first Nazi concentration camp; that the town stands on a hill at the summit of which is the castle of the Wittelsbacher and that the other sight is a parish church (1625).

What *I* remember is driving through sunny fields of potatoes and grain, you watching for road signs and calling the turns (German roads then were still under heavy reconstruction; and one of your frequent bursts of song was *"Umleitung*—there's a muddy road ahead!"). Wasn't my right hand holding your thigh, except when a farmer waved from a yard? Wasn't the town still a village after all, merely houses (no business street that I remember)?—low white houses with small sandy yards, green gardens in front? Don't I remember screened porches, green rockers, dusty ferns in cans, geraniums in boxes? A gray frame railway depot and platform? Didn't I ask to stop and walk awhile or to drive slow and aimless (we had hours till the camp closed) through the loose grid of streets that seemed home at last (were they really unpaved, ankle-deep in white dust?)? But you led us on—"Turn right; here, here." Your unfailing sense of where we were, where we must go. I was ready to wait, stop short of the camp. The village itself, your warm proximity, had eased my urgency for confrontation. What we had—there and then—seemed tested enough by time and chance, to require no further *pro forma* buffeting. It was you—I'm sure of this—who forced us on. An Ariadne who—calm in her beauty, perfectly aware of the course she's set—calmly leads dumb Theseus back into the lethal heart of the maze, its small tidy utterly efficient death chamber, the patient minotaur who has only played possum and waits now, famished.

From the parking lot (!) on—in my memory—it does seem a room, not ample but sufficient and sturdily enclosed. The new small gates (where are the old ones? —*Arbeit Macht Frei*), the cyclone fence thickly threaded with vines, the no-nonsense sign (*Maintained by the Corps of Engineers, U.S. Army*), the clear sky, the light—seemed interior, roofed, sheltered, shrunk or a model scaled precisely to a larger form. Is that why I didn't lock the car?—after weeks of paranoia, left our luggage available to any passer? Or had I started guessing you would stay behind?—guessing and hoping?

You had got yourself out ("Chivalry ends here," you had told me in Stockholm) and stood in sun that suddenly had the weight of sun at home, that seemed each second to be loading you with burdens. Also the color—you were bleaching as I watched. Yet you took off your sunglasses and stood by your shut door, hands at your sides, squinting straight at me.

I came round to you and extended my hand. You accepted. I took a step onward and engaged your weight, gently.

You said "No." You were planted. Your hand stayed in mine but your face refused.

"I said "No, *what?*" and laughed.

"Not going," you said.

I didn't ask why but said what my father always said when I balked—"Are you sick?"

"No," you said.

"Then you promised," I said.

You had not; you should have laughed. But you shook your head.

"If I ordered you?" I said.

"You wouldn't."

"If I did?"

"I wouldn't go."

I said "*Wouldn't* or *couldn't?*"

"Wouldn't," you said.

We had not smiled once!

You took back your hand.

I said "Will you wait?"

You nodded yes.

"Where?"

"I'll *wait*," you said. You half-waved behind you, a cluster of trees, shady grass beneath.

So I moved again to go—to leave in fact—not looking back, and entered the camp. Dachau. Left you waiting, as you chose. Are you waiting still?

You have never seen it and, as I've said, my otherwise sharp pictorial memory is dim on Dachau; so to write this, I've spent three days trailing information through volumes of war-crimes trials, memoirs, histories of the S. S., photographs (forty Jewish women—nude, mostly pot-bellied, three of them holding children— queue up for a massacre in some Polish ditch: two of them are smiling toward the camera). Guess what a good three days I've had—to learn very little more than this (the memoirs on Dachau specifically are in Polish and German, shut to me): Dachau was opened in March 1933, a pet project of Goering and Himmler. The site, a mile square, was equipped for 8,000 inmates. At its liberation in April '45, it contained 33,000—90% civilians, 10% war prisoners. The civilians, from the first, fell into four groups—political opponents, "inferior races" (Jews and Gypsies), criminals, "asocial elements" (vagrants, pimps, alcoholics etc). Further divisions were recognized by the colored patches on prison clothing (selected with a grinning irony)—black for "shiftless elements," yellow for Jews, pink for homosexuals, purple for Jehovah's Witnesses. Though the oldest camp and the popular symbol for all, it was classified in the S. S. scale as a class-I camp—the mildest rating (Auschwitz was III). Only 70,000-odd inmates are estimated to have died there (4,000,000 at Auschwitz). The existing gas chamber was used only experimentally. Indeed, experiment was among the camp's functions—the famous experiments of Dr. Sigmund Rascher in chilling prisoners to 19° C., then attempting to thaw them with live whores stretched on their bodies (Himmler regretted that the chosen whores were Aryan). Or locking prisoners in mock altitude chambers to observe when they'd die of oxygen starvation. Or the study of asepsis by inducing infections which were left to gangrene.

—You know most of that. Everybody over thirty does (though to anyone not there, as prisoner or liberator, it has never seemed credible). What I'd like to tell you is what I saw, twelve years after its liberation. I have the four photographs I took that day. I can build it round them.

The gates were unguarded. I walked through them onto a central road wide enough for trucks but closed now to all but lookers like me—there were maybe a dozen in the hour I was there. To my left, one compound (the only one or the only one saved?)—a four-acre piece of flat tan dirt enclosed by stretches of concrete wall (seven-feet high, electrified on top), relays of barbed wire and, in each corner, an all-weather guardhouse (twenty feet high, all empty now). No trace of barracks, no sign of shelter. Where were the famous "dog cells" in which prisoners could only lie on their sides and were forced to bark to earn their food? Razed apparently (on a partial diagram I count thirty barracks). A few weeds grow and, in my picture of a stretch of wall and guardhouse, a leafy branch decks the upper right sky. (Good composition. But how old is the tree?) No entrance there, no gate in the wire. To the right, though, free access—trees, grass, flowers, buildings.

All the people were there. I remember them as old and all of them women; but my photographs show one man (late forties, his suit and tie American—was he a prisoner here?) and two children under ten (a boy in *lederhosen*, a girl hid behind him)—otherwise, old women in long cheap summer dresses, stout shoes. All in clusters of two or three, simply standing akimbo or reading, their lips moving drily at the effort. There are no talking guides, no sign of a staff to question, only scattered plaques and inscriptions in German—the single attempt at a monument, modest, dignified, undistinguished, a ¾ths-lifesize gaunt bronze prisoner gazing across the road to the compound, head shaved, hands in his scarecrow overcoat, feet in wooden shoes, on his

marble base DEN TOTEN ZUR EHR, DEN LEBENDEN ZUR
MAHNUNG ("To Honor the Dead, To Warn the Living") and an urn of red geraniums. Granite markers
maybe twelve inches square set in beds of geraniums
—GRAB HUNDERTEN NAMENLOSEN (that's from memory
—"Grave of Hundreds, Nameless"; was it *hundreds*
or *thousands?*). Then twenty feet onwards—it is all
so small—six or eight women wait beside a building.
It is one-story, cheap brick, green tile roof, straight as
a box car and only twice as long. At the pitch of the
roof there are turret windows; in the end near me, one
large brick chimney eighteen feet tall. Along the side,
frequent windows and doors. The only sign was a
single black arrow aimed toward the far end (the end
farthest from the compound and hidden). I followed,
past a post-war willow tree, and found at the end a
door—normal size, no wider than the door to my own
bedroom.

From here I am on my own—no pictures. I think I
remember the logic of progression, each small room
labeled in German and English, giving into the next
like a railroad apartment—*Disrobing Room, Disinfect-
ing Room* (roughly ten feet by twelve, nine foot ceilings, unpainted plaster walls scratched now with the
names and hometowns of GI's). Then another nor-
mal-sized wooden door opening into a larger room—
maybe fifteen by twenty, shower spigots, soap dishes,
floor drains, a ceiling window.

—I've built that effect outrageously—I'm sorry—
to the oldest surprise of the twentieth century. The
shower was gas, Zyklon B; the window was a death-
watch; the drains were for hosing down the products of
surprise and suffocation. The next room was small

again—*Storage Room.* The walls were printed from floor to ceiling with dirty bare feet, all turned neatly up. Corpses stacked like cord wood for the ovens. Next room, the ovens. The largest room and last, *Cremato- rium.* Four or five brick ovens spaced six feet apart, their iron doors open on seven-foot grill racks. The walls bore sets of black iron tools—tongs, prods, pokers, shovels. Behind the ovens, in the wall, were little doors —ash chutes to outside, for the *Namenlosen.*

End of tour. No more sights—oh an old woman kneeling by the farthest oven, clicking off her rosary. Otherwise nothing else to linger for but sunlight, gera- niums. Or to make you wait awhile. I thought you were still waiting; and I thought, retracing my way toward you, that I was returning.

You could easily have stood it—have I made you see that? It lacked—now I understand the vagueness of my memories—the mystery of place. There are places, objects, quite literally impasted with the force of past event; places in which one is pulled up short by the pressure of actual atoms of the past. Almost never in America—our shrines being ruthlessly scalded and scoured if not bulldozed—and almost always in sites of suffering or wickedness. The Borgia apartments in the Vatican still are oiled with the presence of Rodrigo Borgia's rotting body; electrons that witnessed, sus- tained, his life still spin in the plaster, the stones underfoot, can be gouged (brown and rank) with a quick fingernail; unaltered atoms of hydrogen and oxy- gen that occupied his holy dissolving lungs in 1495 rush over one's lips and teeth with each breath. Or the Domus Aurea of Nero, subterranean now and leaking, where I rounded a dark corner on an elderly English gentleman masturbating (English by his clothes). Or the dungeon beneath the Capitol in which Caesar strangled Vercingetorix—45 BC. Or—another thing entirely—the crystal reliquary in Santa Maria Maggiore which one Christmas Eve mass was borne toward me, immobile in the crowd, its scraps of wormy wood, whether hoax or not (the remains of the Manger), as immanent with promise and threat to my life as a gram of radium bombarding my eyes. Dachau is one month younger than I. It saw—caused—the agonizing unwilling death of tens of thousands while I was still paying half-fare at the movies; yet its huddled remains bore me less of a threat, less pressure of the past than Williamsburg, than any plastic Hilton lobby.

—Why? That's *my* question. Why was I unshaken, unmoved? Anger with you? Tourist fatigue? (I who could weep years later in Chillon at the pillar to which Byron's Prisoner was chained?—and that after ten days hiking in the Alps.) What had I expected?—a Piranesi prison with eighty-foot ceilings, thick brown air, torture wheels staffed by malignant dwarfs? No doubt that would have helped. The physical remains of Dachau are so mindlessly disproportioned to the volume of suffering they were asked to contain, the literal volume of agonized breath expelled in that square mile in those twelve years. The slaves who died building pyramids are at least survived by pyramids, not tarpaper shacks and geraniums.

But no—don't you see?—I'd expected *home*. It's taken me these twelve years to understand that even— my curious memory (dead-wrong surely) of the town itself as a scene from my childhood (porches, ferns, dust!—eastern North Carolina) and my readiness to

dawdle there with you, my near-panic at the camp gates
when you refused. I had secretly thought through all
those months of planning that this would be our home,
that if we could enter Dachau together, face and com-
prehend its threat and still walk out together, then
we'd be confirmed—a love not soluble in time or death.
Home in the sense of birthplace; we'd have been born
there, our actual marriage, a perfect weld-job in the
ultimate crucible.

Nonsense, you're thinking. Were you thinking it
then? Is it why you refused?—you would not be a party
to soft-brained theatrics?

But surely you're wrong. Sappy as my whole secret
plan may have been—so sappy it was even secret to me;
a Fiery Consummation!—it was not a fool's plan, not
built on lover's lies. I wrote of "comprehending the
threat of Dachau"—hadn't I done that already, in
advance, by insisting on this visit? Its final horror—and
that of all the camps, class I–III—was not the naked
fulfillment by a few thousand gangsters of their fear
and hatred on impotent objects (that, after all, is
everyone's dream) but precisely the threat to human
attachment, loyalty. The ghastliest experiment of all
was not one of Dr. Rascher's mad-scientist pranks but
the high voice that pulsed out its desperate need like a
hypertensive vein—and at first uncertain of its power
to enforce!—"Let me set you apart. Mothers here,
children there. Husbands left, wives right." And millions obeyed, even the de Wieks—the most successful
human experiment in history.

No, the horror is not that the camps did not
revolt, that Treblinka stood alone—the horror was accomplished, ineradicable, the moment any one man

entered Dachau—but that no husbands, wives, parents, children *stood*—by their radios or sofas or milking stools—and said, "No, kill us here in our tracks together." Oh maybe some did—then why are they unknown? Why aren't their statues in every city center, our new saints of love?—so far surpassing Tristan or Abelard or Antony as to burn like constellations over fuming brush fires. We are only left with endless processions of pairs who *agreed*—to abandonment, to separation by other human beings (not death or time). You know that there were mothers who hid from their children on arriving at Auschwitz—buried their own heads in coats or crawled through knees—to escape immediate death? Can they be forgiven that?

Every American over thirty has his favorite obsessive Holocaust story which he's read or, rarely, heard and retails ever after as his version of Hell. An entire sub-study might be done of these stories and their relevance to the teller. I *heard* mine, and after we parted. A colleague of mine—age 38—is a west-Polish Jew. His mother died of TB early in the war. There were no other children and he lived with his father, a practicing dentist. When the roundup came in '42, my friend was eleven. In warm July weather he rode with his father in the packed train to Sobibor—two days, I think, stopping and starting—and once they were there and unloaded on the siding and a doctor came round to eliminate the sick, my friend's father said that his son was consumptive. It was news to my friend; but being a child, he only thought, "Of course he's right; they kept it from me." But his father never touched him and my friend was led off, presumably for gassing or a lethal injection. Some balls-up ensued, his death was delayed;

he never coughed once, chest sound as a stone. But he never saw his father. He was strong enough to work, my friend—farm the camp potatoes—so he managed to live through two more years and a transfer to Auschwitz. Then one day—age thirteen—he was standing in a compound when a line of new men passed. One man fell out for a moment and came toward him. My friend said, "He thought he was running; he was creeping" (too weak to run). Of course, it was his father. They both knew that. But they didn't speak and, again, didn't touch; and a guard beat his father into line—fifteen seconds. Never met again.

Well, in the immortal words of King Lear— "*Howl.*" My friend thinks the question in his story is *why?*—why his father did that. I'd never tell him but the question is *how?* There are degrees of offense at which motive is irrelevant. Can he ever be forgiven?— that father (out of Dante) stumbling on his appallingly vital son whom he'd lied to kill? Can any of the millions ever be forgiven?

Can you, Sara, ever? And not just by me. It was you who refused. Only you were not killed. You could have walked into that tamed camp with me; you could have had the guts to settle it *inside*—to have seen it all with me, to have armed it with the threat which without you it lacked and then (if you needed so desperately) have said to me, "No, I will not live for you." Instead, for your own no doubt clear reasons, you lurked outside on the shady rim, half-sadist, half-coward—unwilling to choose, thinking you could wait and that I, having waited for half an hour beyond a wire fence among debris as meaningless as M. G. M. sets, would presently return.

*   *   *

I did and didn't. When I came back through the gates, I didn't look for you but went to the car and sat in its oven-heat. I already knew that I was not waiting and had not returned, not to you at least; but—stopped short of panic or the courage to act my feeling—I was not prepared to abandon you physically, to leave your bags on the empty parking space and drive off for Salzburg with your twenty-dollar *Figaro* ticket in my wallet. So I thought in the heat, "I may go-under but I won't go looking."

In three or four minutes you walked up slowly, got in and sat, facing forward. How did I feel to you? What vibrations, what aura? Or were you receiving? Had you ever been?

What I felt was hatred. What's *hatred*, you ask? —the wish that you were absent from my sight, my life, absent from my memory. I had put my hands on the wheel for steadiness, and I thought my hatred was shaking the car. Then I saw, in my head, a Volkswagen jittering-away in the sunkist parking lot at Dachau; so I cranked up and moved.

You said "Where are you going?"

I did not want to stop now and look at you—I must keep my hands busy. I said "*I?* To Salzburg."

"Am I coming?" you said.

"Unless you jump," I said.

I think you took that to mean you were forgiven. You behaved as though you were. Slowly through our drive to Salzburg you loosened, slowly became the girl I'd thought I needed—smiles at my profile and, then when we'd got in sight of hills, you sang the whole final scene of *Figaro* (from "*Gente, gente, all'armi, all'armi*"), taking all the parts, chorus included. Your text was letter-perfect, your Italian B+; only your bari-

tone plunges failed. Yet I knew your motive far better
than you. It had nothing to do with the coming evening. It all bloomed out of your need and wish to sing
five lines—

THE COUNT:
>   Contessa, perdono.   [*Countess, your pardon.*

THE COUNTESS:
>   Più docile io sono   —*I'm gentler now*
>   e dico di sì.   *and I'll say yes.*

ALL:
>   Ah! Tutti contenti   —*Ah! Everybody's*
>   saremo così   *happy with that.*]

That, I think, was the climax though the day (and
this piece) had a good while to run. I took that to
mean you were pardoning *me*—for not having cheer-
fully granted your independence back at Dachau, for
not having bought the metaphor your refusal offered
(we'd be hitched to one load but in separate yokes). So
I thought I would launch a spot of unforgivability.
When you'd sung through the orchestral *tutti* to the
curtain, you faced forward resolutely—no bow in my
direction. That meant I should applaud—right? Well,
I drove a good mile before making a sound; and then I
said "One question."

"What?"

"Why in all your extensive *reconciliation* reper-
toire"—can you still do Cordelia, Marina, Fidelio?—"is
it always the *lady* dispensing largess?"

You'd have bit off your tongue before admitting
you hadn't noticed. You said, in an instant, "It's the
way the world's built."

"Many thanks," I said and by then we were threading the fringes of Salzburg, its castle as stunned by the day as I.

I said that this would be my version, what I remember and understand. The rest of the day—what I thought was the day—is necessary; then tell me yours; I genuinely need it. Yet, again, my memory of *places* is vague, my grip on surfaces. You've greased my hands, greased every wall; or is it only some new lubricant from myself, manufactured now in me—suddenly—in response to your refusal, to ease me away? Anyhow, it's still produced. Some days it pours.

Mozart's *Geburtshaus*—we saw that together but what do I recall? Two or three pokey rooms, white walls, dark brown woodwork, an early piano on which (the guide told us) Harry Truman had just played. Was there even a *birth*-room? Were they sure of which room? I couldn't say. It seemed more like the birthplace of some dry chip—say, Metternich—than the Sublime Foul Mouth. And didn't you recognize that? When we'd made our separate rounds and I passed the guest-book on my way downstairs, I saw you'd signed with your comic alter-ego—*Veronica F. Pertle and traveling companion.* We were already lethal, in under three hours—we'd agreed to be a team of cut-rate Midases, transmuting all we touched to chalk.

I slept through a good deal of *Figaro*—all that endless nocturnal business at the start of Act III, the confused identities. I've slept through greater performances than that—Melchior's Lohengrin, Welitsch's Salome—though always before from travel fatigue, biting

off more grandeur than I could chew, but here I wasn't
tired. I'd slept eight hours the night before, driven ten
miles to walk maybe five hundred paces round a concentration camp, then eighty miles farther on a good
wide road. No, I was retreating. The great death wish,
Sleep Mother of Peace—if I couldn't lose you, I could
lose myself. You woke me toward the end with a firm
elbow—"Don't miss the forgiveness." So I can still hear
that (Schwarzkopf's perfect frailty, a bulldozer dis-
guised as a powderpuff); thanks for the elbow—the trip
was not in vain.

What I think I remember—as clear as the Norwegian day, your offered food—is the rest of the night.
Correct me on this—

We had late coffee in some hotel lobby which
seems, in memory, entirely upholstered in 1938 Pontiac
fabric, and were spared conversation by a pair of pur-
ple-haired American ladies drinking *Liebfraumilch* six
feet away. They had also heard the opera and debated
the performance. One defended it stoutly but the
doubter trumped her in the end—remember?—"Ella,
all I know is, when I hear great singing something in
me swells up. Tonight it didn't swell."

—"Mine neither," you said and stood and we left,
heading toward Munich still hungry (no supper). Yet
you didn't mention food, barely spoke at all; and what
did I feel?—that really I was racing, to end this night,
the trip, what we'd had and you'd failed, that I could
go without food and sleep for days, an emergency
encystment for however long it took to deliver you to
whatever door you chose.

Then on the edge of Munich you said, "I'll never
sleep without some food."

It was pushing two a.m. So I had to hunt awhile; but we found a place open somewhere in Schwabing, down a flight of stairs thickly cushioned with dirt.

"More dikes than Holland," you said going in; but in what light there was, they seem more like gypsies to me on hindsight.

You wanted fondue but we settled for something merciful and a good deal of wine; and with all the eating, surely we hadn't said fifty words when the two men entered with the lion before them. If they weren't gypsies I'll surrender my license—they laid down about them that heavy metal air of offense and threat I've known all my life (they still roamed the South when I was a boy, telling fortunes and offering odd skilled services no one would accept, though by then in trailers not painted wagons; and their squat swart women with the Carmen earrings and their men whose hard faces all wore livid scars are high in my childhood pantheon of menace).

They picked you at once. Do you still think I signaled them? I *saw* them see you the moment they entered, even the lion.

He was straining toward you on his red dog-leash —maybe six months old?—and no one held him back though I swear the rear man—the one with hands free —passed the huge lady-owner a small piece of money in their rush to you. Were they illegal, bribing their way? The lion was smelling your foot before you saw; and of course you didn't flinch—a male lion cub in a Bavarian dive at the end of a day comprising Dachau and Mozart: oh.

They were photographers—take your picture with a lion; best American Polaroid, instant result. I told them No—didn't I? I'm almost sure I did—but the contact man (the one with the leash) held the lion up and said "See, he *begs*." With his free hand he clasped the cub's front paws together in a mockery of prayer (its high tight testicles were pink as salmon, utterly vulnerable). The man's English seemed more Italian than German but maybe just basic PX English—"He begs you to warm him; four dollars for picture, give to your husband. He lose his mother, he lonely here." The cub's eyes were shut, so lonely he was dozing.

You continued eating but you asked him "Did you kill her?"

That seemed the terror-button. Surely these two oily small-time spivs had not been poaching in Kenya; yet at your question, they both threw grimaces at one another, and the talker said, "Look. No charge for you." He extended the lion, eyes still shut—"He need your help."

"He's asleep," you said.

The man jogged him hard; he looked out, groggily.

"No," you said.

But I said "Do it" and produced my wallet. I wanted you to do it and I wanted to pay.

Looking at the lion not me, you said "Why?"

"I want the picture."

I extended twenty marks to the man and you stood.

"You sit," the man said, "then we take you both."

"I'll stand," you said. "It's me he wants." You stood and reached out. You were in the black dress with narrow shoulder straps—much white skin showed.

He moved close against you and hung the lion on your shoulder like a child. The photographer—the si-

lent man—backed off and raised his camera; the talker
said "Big smile."

You smiled sideways, no teeth. The other diners
paused, awaiting the flash. It came. In its light, blood
streamed down your arm.

The lady-owner bellowed, came waddling forward.
The two men leapt toward you. The lion was clamped
into the meat of your shoulder.

I was still in my chair.

"Stay back," you said.

They understood and stopped a foot from the
table.

"What's his name?" you said.

The talker said "Bob."

The lady-owner babbled coldly in German. They
must get him out, get out themselves, *die Polizei!*

You were stroking the back of Bob's locked-on
neck, simply saying his name again and again—the two
of us the only calm people in the room, only still ones
at least. Us and the lion—he was motionless, teeth
deep in you. What nourishment was he taking?—what
pleasure, fulfillment? What did he think you were?

—A lion-tamer, anyhow. You stroked him free; he
looked round at his owners. You had never smiled,
talked baby-talk to him, given the odor of fear or asked
for help; you had saved your day. You handed Bob over
to the trembling talker.

He slapped him once across the nose, laid my
money by my plate; and they left at a trot—the owner
behind them, maledicting.

(*I don't have the picture.* Have you thought of
that? Did we ever mention that? Of course, I didn't pay
but a picture was taken, at the instant of the bite. Does

it still exist in some gypsy's pocket?—an image of a bad
night, another close call, image of his *life*, assault and
impotence, the helpless witness of another's competence to solve hurtful puzzles? I would give a lot for it.
What is on your face?—still, after twelve years? What
did I miss in the moment of flash, your moment of
sudden unexpected pain? Whom were you blaming? I
need that picture badly.)

Before I could stand up to check the damage, you
had asked a bystander, "*Wo ist die Damen?*" and loped
off to that.

So I sat again and was wondering what next when
the owner pounded back with a rusty first-aid kit and
stopped at me, aghast.

"*Wo ist ihre Gattin?*"

I said that the *Fraulein* was in the cabinet, washing.

She considered attempting to wither me for negli-
gence but no doubt remembered that in her situation
die Polizei was a two-edged blade; so she said, "*Nicht
toll, nicht toll. Er ist nicht tollwütig*" (*not rabid*) and
headed for the *Damen* to disinfect you.

I ate on and in five minutes she returned to say
you were all right, would be back soon and would we,
in recompense, have a free dessert? I thought that
seemed uniquely German—for a lion-bite, dessert—but
I accepted and she quickly produced two enormous
wedges of obscenely moist chocolate whipped-cream
cake. I thanked her, she assured me again "*Nicht toll*"
and that you were fine. Then she left.

I waited awhile—thinking what? Most likely,
nothing. (I can sit for whole half-hours, thinking nothing, my consciousness a bowl of thick soup, cooling.

You'd never accept that; so often, on the road, when we'd ridden in silence, you'd say "What are you think-ing?" and when I'd say "Nothing," you'd clearly dis-believe me. *Why?* What mutterings filled *your* silence? It is how I understand the life of objects. Keats said that he could inhabit a sparrow and peck in the gravel. I can inhabit, say, a walnut log or the white blind heart of a loaf of bread.) Maybe though I thought a few calm sad thoughts on our imminent split—*past* split, in fact; it was hours old. But I know I wasn't yet asking *why?* I was now an engine geared for one purpose—the expul-sion of waste parts, self-starting restored. And when, in five minutes, you hadn't come, I began my cake and called for coffee. In ten more, I'd finished; you were still absent; and the owner walked past me—no word or look—to check you again.

She returned and I managed to understand through her fury that now you had the outer door locked and had spoken to her but would not open.

I couldn't think of how to say "Give her time"; so I must have stared blankly till the owner said in Eng-lish in a python-hiss (discovering *Ssss* in two *s*-free words)—"Go. *You* go!" She'd have punched me in the breast bone with her short fat finger, but I leaned back and stood and went to the *Damen*.

I knocked and called your name.

You must have been against the door—no sound of steps—but you took a few beats before turning the lock.

When I opened, you were standing three feet away, by a grimy wash basin, your back to me, your head down but silent.

I said "Are you hurt?"

You turned to show me. Your face was splotched from crying; but you weren't using that—no mercy pleas. You pointed to your shoulder. One single strip of bandage, one inch by two.

I looked from where I was—I'd entered entirely but the door was cracked open (for needy *Damen*). It didn't occur to me to take another step, touch you gently, peel the bandage back and check—was that all my fault? Weren't you throwing off a field of volts that I'd never have pierced, however determined?

"One tooth," you said, "one canine puncture."

"Good," I said. (I knew you'd had tetanus shots and, now from the owner, that Bob was not rabid.)

You said it to my eyes (I grant you that), "*Good?* Well, I guess"—another three beats, no shifting of gaze —"Yes, *marvelous*. Something *in* me finally. And a permanent mark." You pressed the bandage. "I'll carry a little white scar to my grave, the size of a navy bean—a real lion, my summer in Europe. I can show my children." You reached for your purse and, as you came toward me, said "Chocolate on your teeth" (was I grinning by then?). Then you said, "I need air. Please wash your mouth and I'll meet you at the car." You went out past me, half-closing the door again.

So since the room was empty I went to the basin. In the mirror I seemed unaltered though my teeth were socketed in chocolate. I was flushing my mouth when (I never told you) I saw your little message—to the side of the mirror and in small printed letters but quite clearly your hand (the only graffito, your color of ink, of course in English). Before I could read it, I knew it was not for me. You'd had no way to know I'd enter the *Damen*—or had you? did you wait to force me to

come and see the two lines? Is it why you wouldn't let
the owner in? How could she have minded? She'd have
never understood. Who on God's earth would?—

> *Jesus, will you help me now?*
> *I will. I have.*

I thought at once of Salinger's *Franny*—mystical
union in the Ladies Room—but I knew that, even if
you'd read the story you'd have thought it unforgivably
corny to mimic its action, like quoting Edgar Guest at
a family funeral. In any case, Franny only squeezed her
little book, *The Way of the Pilgrim*; you addressed
Jesus straight and claimed a straight answer. You were
surely not drunk, surely not joking. I dreaded facing
you. What help had you got? What new fierce power?
How much farther could you thrust me?

But I went, paid the bill, thanked the owner for
her help and the chocolate cake—she smiled but
despised me—and climbed to the street.

The car was parked five steps away—no sign of
you. I looked toward both dark ends of the street—
nothing, empty. I stood yearning to run—to enter the
car silently, crank and drive away. You had your pass-
port and traveler's checks. And I'd taken a step—would
I have done it?—when you rounded the nearest corner,
stopped in the cone of light. I waited for you to come
on to me.

But you pointed behind you down the hidden
street and held your place.

So I went to you, more curious now than dreading.
You were back in darkness before I reached you—I was
both spared and deprived full sight of your face.
"You're all right?" I said.

You didn't answer that. You pointed again toward the end of the street—what seemed a small park, a knot of trees.

I said, "Do you want to walk?"

You said, "No, I've got something to show you."

I walked beside you but you were leading.

The park was two concentric rings of sycamores that all but filled the dark space above with limbs, leaves. Only a piece of sky twenty feet square, say, was visible; but despite the glow of Munich and the few park lights, there were stars—oh a dozen. You took us to the center.

I looked round—alone; all benches empty.

Then you said "Straight up!"

I looked, half-thinking you had lost a screw; even one-tenth wondering if you'd stab my unprotected gut (you who trapped spiders in my Oxford rooms and conveyed them, live, outside to grass).

Again you were pointing. "See those two stars there?"

"Yes."

"Now shift to the right and down an inch or so."

I did.

"See that blur?"

I waited, straining not to blink; then I saw it—a faint smear, an old chalk fingerprint. "Yes."

You moved closer on me and, there as I was, hands loose at my sides, head back, throat stretched taut, I considered again that you might have plans and means to kill me—a sacrifice to what? Your Jesus-of-the-*Damen?* Some Eastern star god?—Ishtar, Ahura Mazda? For that moment, it seemed an acceptable fate—or not to over-dignify it, *acceptable next act*, Tosca and Scarpia, *finalmente mia!* (Is it from this whole full day that my total fearlessness emerges? Death would startle me, granted, but roughly as much as an air-filled bag popped behind my ear. I face all prospects quite nicely, thank you; let Nothing mishear me though and apply misfortunes.)

But you only spoke. "Do you know what it is?"

I said "Do you?"

"NGC 224."

"Is that a space ship?" I said (no satellites yet, though the Russians were cranking up, a little to our right).

"No, the great spiral galaxy in Andromeda."

I had vague recollections of boyhood astronomy, photographs in *My Weekly Reader* from Mount Palomar; but I certainly made no leap of awe.

You said, "Do you know how far away it is?"

"No."

"One million, five hundred thousand light years. And what its apparent diameter is?"

"No," I said.

"Sixty thousand light years." Your hand was still up, no longer quite pointing but in a sort of arrested Boy Scout salute; and your lips were parted—you were just beginning.

Yet my dread, such as it was, was ebbing. The worst possibility now seemed clearly nothing more than a Thornton Wilder sermon on Just-us and the Stars— you *were* drunk, I thought; this was way below standard.

You dropped your hand but continued silently looking up.

So I felt I had to speak. "What am I supposed to do?"

"Forgive me," you said.

That was meant to be worse than a sacrificial knife. It was. I must have wobbled. At some point I said "For what?" I was facing you now—or your dim profile; you would not look downwards.

"You know," you said.

"For waiting back today at Dachau?"

"More than that," you said.

"Say what then, please."

"For not thinking you were safe to follow."

"Into poor Dachau? It's a national park. There are not even bears."

"Don't joke. *You* know."

I didn't know but I didn't ask—because, just then, I didn't want to know and, after the whole day, couldn't care much. Simple as fatigue.

You apparently knew—had thought through your balking and, in asking for pardon, were asking your way back into my life. I was safe, after all, to follow?—was that it? Or safe as you guessed you could hope to find? Or maybe you'd realized after all that you'd led, not followed, all those years in any case?

I wasn't standing there, in silence, asking questions —again I was locked in simple fatigue.

Then you looked at me and said "You haven't answered."

"What?" I said.

You said again "Forgive me?"

I should have said Yes. It was surely the instinct, the reflex of my feeling; but with Yes in my mouth, I balked and thought, "I must wait till tomorrow. It would be my tiredness talking, and the wine." It would —I know now—have been my heart but wait I did. I said "Give me time."

You nodded, gave it and went to the car only slightly before me.

But in two further weeks on the road, I never answered. (Not that I forgot; it was all I thought of—a glaze of scum which I laid across all those Rembrandts and Vermeers that might have saved us if they'd cared enough to fight. They survived it though, my self-surrendered vandalism. You and I didn't, no masterworks.) And you never asked again. You should have. Why not? You had led so much of the way. Your silence and patience only fueled my flight, stoked a natural warmth of sadism in me which let me ride beside—*lie* beside you—for weeks more and still wish that you would vanish, speaking civilly but coolly, touching you only by accident. (If you were awake— and I did wait until you were breathing like sleep—I beg your pardon now that twice in those last weeks I lay beside you, not ten inches away, and took what pleasure my head demanded from my own dry self with my own dry hand: dry to keep the slapping down. Fun, fun.)

Why? You never asked that even. Why, after years of assuming I required you—daily sight of you, daily touch—after gladly embracing the prospect of *life* with you, your one false move in the parking lot at Dachau thrust me from you in a helpless irresistible rush? Worse than helpless, *grinning*. I was glad, I thought, to go. Blessed clear space at hand—empty, free—toward which I flew at stunning speeds like your galaxy.

Well—Jesus—we've uncovered the secret of Dachau, of all the camps, every act of submission, why no

one refused, even the de Wieks—they were glad to go!
In secret glee, which they could not have borne to face
or seek themselves, millions like us were permitted to
abandon all human contracts, bonds—*duties!*—to shed
all *others* like last year's skin and to stand, if only for a
few hours, free; breathing free air (unshared by wives
or children) till the air became gas. There were two
women smiling in that photograph, remember? holding
their children for the last heavy moment before pitch-
ing forward, dead in a ditch, but alive maybe one
moment longer than the child. After such knowledge,
what forgiveness? We should never have acquired it, by
chance or intent. Yet you forced it on us—by your
simple refusal twelve years ago at Dachau.

I'm back where I started, Sara—why did you refuse?

Never mind. I won't care now. But one more
thing—your astronomy lecture, so unheralded that
night in the Munich park, when I thought you'd gone
nuts if not homicidal (messages from Jesus and NGC
224)? I've been working on that lately—what you
might have intended, short of an open-air homily on
the need for love in the drowned depths of space. I've
read up on your pet galaxy Andromeda—Fred Hoyle,
the *Larousse Astronomie*, even old Sir James Jeans'
Mysterious Universe with its chilling, exhilarating, un-
answerable conclusion—

> *We discover that the universe shows evidence*
> *of a designing or controlling power that has*
> *something in common with our own indivi-*

dual minds—not, so far as we have discovered, emotion, morality, or aesthetic appreciation, but the tendency to think in the way which, for want of a better word, we describe as mathematical. And while much in it may be hostile to the material appendages of life, much also is akin to the fundamental activities of life; we are not so much strangers or intruders in the universe as we at first thought. Those inert atoms in the primaeval slime which first began to foreshadow the attributes of life were putting themselves more, and not less, in accord with the fundamental nature of the universe.

Were you making one last try, that night, to accord us with the universe?

I've bought its picture—your galaxy's. After years of wondering and stumbling across it, badly printed and dingy, in various books, I ordered its photograph from Mount Palomar. For two weeks now it's hung above my desk—only just below Jesus, your other messenger (Rembrandt's Hundred Guilder print, in a first-class fake). So it watches me this minute (as it watches perpetually, day-sky or night). The picture (through the 48" Schmidt telescope) is in color—the great spiral itself in white, rose and lilac on a matte brown sky pierced by single stars. If I didn't know, it could be several things—a Miami lady-decorator's dream of the ultimate ballroom chandelier. Or—for me most pleasing—the loveliest toy ever made. It could be that (sixty thousand light-years across)—a cooling circular platter of light that whirls round its billowing center in utter

silence, having no final rim but diminishing slowly into
thinner clouds of stars and finally night; my dream of a
mobile to hang in my bedroom to wake to at night; or
the sort of gift that God the Father might have willed
for the Infant Christ (trumping the Magi) in a Milton
ode (what if Milton could have seen it?)—

And for a sign of My delight in Thee,
I hang this tilted wheel above Thy bed,
Attended at the rim by Hosts who smile
And, smiling, face the axle drowned in light
Whence My eternal love for Thee streams fire.

Did we really see it that August night? Was that
smudge above Munich really it? Or were you lying? Or
did you not know? I haven't yet found in any of my
reading whether or not the Andromeda galaxy is visible
ever to the naked eye—and if so, was it visible in
Munich that particular night (or early morning)?

Look. I'm going to assume that you really thought
you saw it and that—calling me and pointing up and
reeling off those almanac-facts as prelude to asking
forgiveness—what you meant to say was something like
this, another effort at the poem you were always aching
to write (your poem, not mine; mine would be better
but that's my job, right?)—

There it hangs, a million and a half light years
away, sixty thousand visible light years across, com-
posed of billions of separate stars all drowned in
isolation yet all wheeling round a common center
at something like a half million miles per hour, a
stroke of radiance on your retina dimmer than the
luminous dial of your watch. Or there it hung *a*

million years ago, for the instant it took to launch
this present light in its unimaginable outward
flight toward the curved walls of space. Flight
from what though?—the Big Bang? Maybe. But..
maybe flight from us, simply you and me, the two .
repellent objects at the core of space from which
all other matter hurtles at speeds increasing till
they pass the speed of light (and hurtled for millions of years before us in anticipation of this one
day). Or a little less narcissistically—in flight from
the blue planet, home of men. For elsewhere, all
creatures desire perfect union—desire not require
—and each one's desire is silently achieved. Paral-.
lels meet. It is how the world is made. Andromeda
—the millions of other universes, the billions of..
planets—is swarmed with pairs who serve each
other. Or, barring that, is empty; has the grace to
be empty. We will not be forgiven for forcing their
flight. Turn. Return.

I'd add only this—it is all no doubt grander, fun-
nier than that. God only watches comedies, can only
smile. Waterloo, Dachau. The end is planned. There
are no options.

Sara, come back.

T W O

ELEGIES

Late Warnings

MY PARENTS, WINTER 1926

THE KNOWLEDGE OF MY MOTHER'S
COMING DEATH

LIFE FOR LIFE

DESIGN FOR A TOMB

Invitation, for Jessie Rehder

Summer Games

LATE WARNINGS

My parents, winter 1926

MY PARENTS—not yet my parents—stand on a crude plank bridge. The sky behind them is bleak, trees bare—November, December 1926. (My mother's left hand proves the year no later. She casually hides it —no wedding ring yet. They will marry soon, deeper into winter, January.) But they wear no more than their Sunday suits (his black or blue, hers tan or gray); no overcoats, scarves, boots or gloves. My father's hat is in his hand. My mother's shoes are baby-doll slippers. Her spit-curl rests on her forehead, no wind. Yet the day is clearly cold—the air, the light. Late afternoon, by its slant.

They are unprotected. They do not feel cold. They lounge, unshuddering, loose in their clothes; stock-still for the camera.

Or perhaps they do not care but only yearn—to touch entirely. They have not, will come to their wedding as virgins (so my father believed). Then how can they stand so calmly at ease and smile so slightly at their cameraman? (Does he offer some threat?) My father's eyes smile inward only (his goal in sight, his five years' courtship now promised reward); my mother's only smiling is expressed in her stance—she cants herself confident against my father's shoulder, down his whole left side.

They must care, must quickly protect themselves. Take shelter in time.

They will not—did not, perhaps by then could not. And shelter from what?

Where, for instance, is my father's left leg? Why does their shadow not resemble them?

The Knowledge of My Mother's Coming Death

Saturday

OUR meetings now are allegorical. Each week I
haul my soiled clothes thirty miles—my house to
hers. Each week she brings them clean—her house
to mine. This afternoon in May we meet at mine. She
sits before my window in my new chair—its saddle-
brown obscured by her blue dress, her gray hair
streaked by green light off my trees. I face her from the
sofa, near enough—she sees me best at three-yards
distance now. We talk of daily things—her car, my
leaking roof—as one man's hands might speak to one
another, thirty-two years of mutual life between them
or like cooled lovers, joined but satisfied. I even roam
her face, discovering beauty—the dark gold eyes, the
open smiling mouth (spread wings but resting)—all as
familiar as if I had made it. I partly have. All but the
neat scar railing down her forehead, one inch behind
which beat two aneurysms, bared two years ago but
covered at once, untouched and lethal. Her time-bomb,
she calls it—who knows the time? But not today. Not
now it seems. We are spared again. The sun is in the
window now, behind her. She is bright. She turns from
me an instant. The line of her features transmits warm
light. Her face has assumed the translucence of age—
youth and age—and I think inside my own sound head,
"I have loved you all your life," then remember she
lived twenty-seven years before starting me. Still I do
not feel I have lied or blubbed. She says "Four-thirty"

and faces me. She must start home before the evening
rush; so I end on money, as I mostly do—but offering
not asking. Proud as a camel (her bank account under
twenty dollars) she smiles, "Not now. Save till I'm
needy." —"But you'll let me know?" —"I'll let you
know. When I need anything I'll call on you." We
walk to her car. She says, "I'll see you when your
clothes are dirty." I offer again what I've offered before
—to take the clothes to a laundry here, spare her the
chore. I intend both kindness and separation. She rec-
ognizes both, accepts the first, laughs, "And put a fat
blind sixty-year-old widow out of work?"—"No," I say.
She says, "You hate this. I know you do." I look up
rebuked but she means her car—its color, milk-green. I
do, I forgot. "I forgive it," I say.—"Thank you," she
says, smiles, we kiss, she starts. Her car snaps smartly
down my drive. She does not look back. I watch her
dust as she reaches the road, is consumed by leaves;
think, "The best woman driver in history"; then suddenly know, not coldly nor in fear but know for the
first time without the least doubt—"That is the last
sight I have of her."

Sunday

I KNOW it is day but I still lie dreaming, the
frail quick thread that races morning—scraps of
rhyme, clever retorts, problems dispatched. Then I
calm, fall awhile; fall slower, slower till in stillness I
endure this knowledge: my mother and I move in her
car (whose color I no longer hate) through the heart of
a city. She drives as always effortlessly, the visible sign
of her inner grace. I sit on her right in a passenger's

daze. She stops for a light and another car stops on her side, close beside her. The passenger in that car is a girl age twenty. She could easily touch my mother's face, its left profile; but instead she stares and I watch her stare. It slowly becomes a crouch, a frown, then a silent scream. The light goes green. My mother shifts gear, moves forward first, proceeds through the junction, continues her way. Yet terror is stuck in my chest, a stob. I study what half of her face I can see—the right profile, unchanged, at work. I know what waits on the left side though—the girl's frown has only confirmed my knowledge. I say "Mother" calmly—"Look here at me." Half-smiling she looks full-face a moment—the time she can spare from the road—and I see my oldest fear enacted. The artery beneath her left profile presses forward—a tree. A bare purple tree, rocks forward, peels downward silently. I think, "She is dying. I must take the wheel." But she faces the road, still efficient though dead, bearing me forward—her urgent task.

I wake, the stifling weight of dread. At breakfast I down the impulse to phone her; but by noon when I still have not thrown the dream, I drive ten miles to visit a friend, then do not tell him, sit gray and quiet in his room a bombsite, he whole at its center laughing on. At last he says, "What has ruined your day?" I say, "I have dreamt my mother's death." He takes an unseen world for granted (battles it daily), says "That would ruin it."

Monday

THAT friend is with me at my house now. He sits in the new chair and I sit opposite. The doors are open to the loud spring night. We laugh against it, then are suddenly silent—a natural pause. But the night has paused with us, entirely still; and in that silence (two seconds at most) a tide turns against us, against the house. The night lunges brute at every opening, every dark pane. We two seem under crushing assault, hopeless, surrendered. I look to him, look first to his hands —broad, knob-knuckles; they are gripped to the sides of the chair, blood gone. His face looks to me from the pitch of a shudder. He is bearing the brunt. Then the surge subsides; first from me, more slowly from him. We sit a moment exhausted, grateful. Then I half-laugh, say toward him "What happened?"—"Nothing," he says. I have not guessed but I know he lies. And now I cannot accept a lie. I say, "But it did—and to you. What happened." He does not—cannot? will not?—face me. "Not *happened*," he says. "It has not happened yet."

Not yet but will. I am sure now of waiting.

Tuesday

I HAVE eaten my supper, stacked the three dishes. In an hour I must drive ten miles, a meeting. The trip takes less than twenty minutes; but I start to go now, pulled out of the house by my ancient fear of missing things—trains, friends, the smallest chance. I wrench on a tie, rush into my coat, take a single step from closet to door. The phone rings. Now. Do I know? Have I learned? No. The instant of fright, leap of response are my constant reactions to telephone bells —that all news is bad. I stop its ring, pause before

Hello, embracing the silence. A strange woman's voice, "Is this Mr. Price?"—"Yes," I say. She does not name herself—"I am here at your mother's . . ."

I have not learned from the three past days but now I know. I silently recite in unison with her— "Something has happened to your mother." —"I know." —"You know? It only just happened." —"I mean that I know what has happened," I say. "Where is she now?" —"The ambulance has just left for Wake Hospital." —"Thank you," I say, "I will go straight there." I lower the phone, hear her speak against extinction, raise it again, take the explanation this stranger must give. She inhales deeply—"Reynolds" (awards me my first-name, consolation), "she was talking on the telephone, sitting in this chair where I am now. I was across from her, saw it all. She stopped herself in the midst of a sentence, put her right hand to her forehead slowly, looked at me and said, 'I have a terrible pain in my head.' Then she dropped the phone and looked at her lap and began to pick at the nap of her skirt as if it was stain. Then she slumped on herself so I went to her. You don't know me but I . . ."

I thank her, say I am on my way. Then in cold efficiency (a gift from my dream) I call the hospital emergency room. A woman answers. I give my name, say, "My mother is on her way to you now. She cannot talk, will be unconscious and I want to warn you what to expect. She has had two cerebral aneurysms for some years now. They are on either side of the optic chiasma. One was ligatured two years ago with a Crutchfield clamp. The other has burst." —"All right," she says, "we'll be looking for her." I say, "I am coming there now myself." "All right," she says—then, "Are you a

doctor?" —"No," I say. —"You sound like a doctor."
—"No," I say. —"You know so much I thought you
must be." She intends it as compliment, has time to
talk on —"How do you know so much?" she says. I
tell her, "I keep my eyes very clean," then am seized in
a scalding strangling shudder, set the phone in its
cradle, say aloud to the room, "What do I know, what
will anyone know who cannot, will not read plain
warnings; who if I could read, could still not save my
love from death?—save her skull slowly filling itself,
a bowl of blood?"

Life for Life

SIFTING the debris of my mother's death—Death
Mother of Trash (old bank books, canceled checks)—
my numb hands find an emblem of her life, a stack of
records (brittle 78s) which I have not played through
in twenty years, island planted by her in her death,
pleasant garbage to relieve my chore. I rock back on
numb haunches, smile, suck breath (hot July breath),
then lift the records to a cooler room, unlid the old
Victrola, throw its switch. Like every other thing here
now she's dead, it leaps to duty; eager, accurate spins. I
pile on half the stack, fall heavily into my father's chair
still dark with his head oil, he dead ten years, surrender
to the waiting random order—hoot of Emmy Destinn
as Mignon, Lucrezia Bori's lean *Vedrai carino*; then
suddenly as bombs within the room, the forties: Spike
Jones' *Chloe*, crash of kitchens (through laughter,
crash of Warsaw, London, Frankfurt); then Franklin
Roosevelt, 1941, the 8th December, "I ask the Congress to declare . . ." At thirteen on my own I sent for
this, from N. B. C., a birthday gift for Father. Half-
pained, half-peeved, I rise, reject it harshly. Still covered by one more, the next disc falls, clatter of changer,
roar of needle, voice—"Good morning, Mrs. Jones. My
name is Price. I've come to show . . ."

My father's voice. Forgotten. Lost. Now round me
in his room. Slow, calm—the only music he could

make. Twenty-one years of daily hearing it; but ten
years gone, I could no more have heard it in my head
than Lincoln's voice—have often tried at night to
dredge it back, send it looping through some favorite
joke, some mimic, even to bear again its last few words
(nonsense fierce as flail across my eyes, gargled from
cancerous lungs through silver tube). But here again I
have him and remember. A demonstration record made
by him in 1940 when he had sold more toasters, fans,
lamps, stoves than any other salesman in the state and
as reward was asked to speak his pitch in lasting wax
(*reward* when he was locked in blank torment—down-
ing his thirst to drink, drown finally, and baffled to find
ten simple dollar bills to meet this month's new howling creditor).

I down my own new need to stop him. I grant him
the rest of his respite, reward.

". . . Mrs. Jones, do you know that many children" (*chirren* he says) "will suffer poor eyes in years
to come just because of the light they study by?" (His
just is *jest*.)

I had even lost that!—the *jest* that littered his life,
every speech of the thousands he for years unreeled on
the stoops of strangers, incurious, ungrateful—merely
and rightly bored, whole lives being daily laid at their
feet, reeled out from twitching guts like garden hose,
the past shames, present needs of grinning beggars.
Postman, parents, lovers, mirrored selves.

"Now Mrs. Jones, if you will say the word, I'll
bring you on approval our new floor lamp. No obliga-
tion on your part at all . . ."

I say the word she never can, calm No, and end his
endless bottled plea for hope. Next record plays, bald

irony, black jest, Anderson sings *Komm Süsser Tod* of Bach.

So Father, sweet death I have given you, mere silence, rest; vowed not to force you through your pitch again. To seal the vow I look up to your picture on the wall. Deep walnut frame, deep window on your face. 1918, you eighteen yourself, the worst of wars hung bleeding overhead (your brother Edward's lungs already gassed; your own Guard button in your left lapel, an eagle spread above a waiting world; you will be called-for weeks from now yourself but saved in port by Armistice) and still your gaze though high is clear, undoubting; a surety that even now seems firm, not boyish foolishness, seems well-informed as though you saw sure detailed happy futures, a life like water (clear, needed, useful, permanent, free), spared all you will so soon acquire (drink, wife, sons, labor, thirty-six more years). I touch the glass above your silent mouth, say silently—

Dear boy (dear gray eyes, broad nose, curling lip), locked on your browning cracking paper card, I offer you my life—look, it will serve. Cancel all plan of me, let me not be, so you may have free time, move always sure, accept with smooth hands what your eyes still see, elude brute ambush of your gurgling death.

Design for a Tomb

AMONG the things modern sons are spared are
parental tombs—the bother, the crippling expense, the
arrangements to find space, an artist; then choose a
design that will honor the dead with a minimum of gas,
guard their alarmingly indestructible bones and yield to
any thoughtful stranger some sense of the lives discon-
tinued within.

The job now is simple as buying a dog—a burial
plot 18′ × 12′ at the cost of Manhattan real estate; a
tasteful stone with the names blown in by compressed
air through rubber stencils, as ruthless in placement as
neon light.

I've bought you that. Mother bought it, in fact, at
Father's death, ruinous as a pyramid—$600, consuming
what insurance the cancer had spared—but I chose the
design, remembering his wish of nine years before to
have a gravestone like FDR's. Not quite the tonnage
Hyde Park could bear but the principle, at least—two
marble slabs, unveined Vermont white, one flat, one
standing, PRICE the one interruption of the perfect
planes since fouled by birds and blundering mowers yet
broad enough to straddle the four of us.

But suppose I had not and the choice was now
mine, to cover you both with whatever was due—un-

limited funds and artists at hand. (I recall Father laughing two dozen times that when Mother died, he'd set over her "a Coca-Cola and a pack of BCs in Georgia granite." She'd rally, "I'll pile a little hill on you; name it Worry Wart.")

An allegory—*Grief?* (which I no longer feel); my own bust weeping, my brother grim beside me? *Generosity?*—a pair of hands, open? An eternal flame?—in Carolina summers? with Father fire-phobic?

—Your faces of course. The Greeks, again—faces are what we succeed in making (barring burns, cuts, pox, enemies with blades); triumph or mess, our one *personal* product. Therefore tombs should be portraits —smooth runner or bride taken young, gravely vapid; wife, husband, parent. The unique face, the hair often mantled—in prospect of journey—an arm almost always crooked toward the shoulder, palm toward the eyes. "Farewell?" or "Follow me"?

I'd set over you your faces—coarse stone, veined, soluble in time—your bodies to the waist; arms down however (you have not beckoned me, or have only begun).

But your faces when?

—Not in grace of youth (which I never saw) nor as stunned by your endings but as, say, six weeks before your deaths you met your days (work, sons, selves) filled, runnelled, pouched with all you'd learned—self-steerage, laughing charity, as yet unappalled by your readiness to die.

INVITATION

for Jessie Rehder   1908–1967

T<small>HE GIFTS</small> that you gave me (*presents*, not *love*
nor entire *loyalty*; they were daily issue) were few and
small (we all laughed—you hardest—at your chinchery)
—from your Caribbean Christmas, a dishtowel-map
of the West Indies; from your California summer, a
butcher's apron; from my last sight of you, a white
hyacinth. (My thirty-fourth birthday. You'd called me
to your house, too low to visit me; and when I'd gone,
climbed your yard—littered now—and found you
hunched at the living-room table, stroking accurate as a
rhino at a paint-by-number canvas of yellow roses, and
when you'd stood to show the pounds you'd lost since
your little heart spell—slacks and jersey flapped round
you, an idle tent—when you'd shown me your face
bound for death like a ship, then you said "Many
more!" and gave me my present—a hyacinth blooming
in a cardboard pot. Did you see?—as I did at once—the
petals were browning, the odor a furious final exhaling?
Yet it outlasted you by a week of warm days; and its
dry leaves are out my kitchen window now, bulb com-
mitted to my hard starved garden.)

But the two emblems of you which I possess
(which, barring fire, will outlast me though their mean-

ing may not) were not gifts but begged—I pestered you
for them. Two photographs. The first of you at about
twenty-three (say, 1930; three years before my birth).
We came across it in your crammed scrapbooks one
hot night last summer on your plastic sofa (after cold
crab salad and peach ice-cream which, since we survived, surely showed us immortal). I was shocked by its
sudden still loveliness among all your decades of prank-
shots, gags (you a Viking chief in your senior play, you
in rhinestones and tank-suit on the Riviera, you at
ninety-five pounds after your breakdown, in a ballet
pose—a camera was your signal for self-vandalism);
and I said with our usual tactlessness, "You were lovely,
Jessie," then bit my tongue. —"*That* day," you said. "It
was Aunt Mary's fault. She had found me a husband, a
millionaire widower. He'd never seen me and this picture was meant to be his first look. Aunt Mary worked
on my wardrobe for days, would dress me like a doll,
then strip me, try again—new coat, hat, scarf; best
photographer in town, shot through foggy lenses, all
haze and glow. Then I saw the proofs and stopped her
there, wouldn't let her contact her rich prospect."—
"But why?" I said. You studied the face—"She had
covered me up." She had—silk scarf to your chin; soft
Garbo hat shading all your high forehead, half your
huge right eye. You peer from a cave and, shyly but
firmly and permanently, you issue your message and
invitation—*I will come, for the asking, to your generous heart; be your laughing servant as long as I live.* No
takers, not one. And the last day I saw you, you knew
that at last. Your terrible offer was down; gate had
crashed. Now we talked through a grill, you unlikeliest
of cloistered nuns; I what?—parent, friend, lover,
gently abandoned? Both of us free *and* sentenced now

—you to your death in less than two days, propped
reading in bed, the maid five steps away unwarned
(autopsy found no cause—blood, lungs, veins entirely
clear; heart simply reneged) and I to what?

—To, among unknowns of time and face, the
other picture I begged from you, other message you
grudged me. A blurred Kodachrome from your summer
in France two years ago; from a Norman church, a
peeling mural, four figures from a medieval Dance of
Death—two elegant skeletons, wasp-waisted, prancing;
between them two persons. A tall stout lady entirely in
red—red cloak to the throat, red wide-brimmed hat, red
veil round her face (an abbess? in red?) and a gray
young man; face, cap, doublet, hose one shade of gray.
Each is attended by a skeleton, is gripped at the wrist
by an icy bone. Each gestures with the free hand, palm
upraised—not a frantic "No" but a calm "Not yet." In
vain. The forward rhythm is set. Their feet are perform-
ing what their hands refuse. You had had this enlarged
for your living-room wall. I asked for a print. You
firmly said "No." The request had been idle, my answer
unthinking—"Tightwad," I said, "I'll gladly pay."—
"Not that," you said, "Ask for anything else—take the
leopard skin." So, baffled now and mildly peeved, I
dropped the request. But a few days later you brought
me my print, much smaller than yours (half-a-dollar
saved!), laid it on my sofa with no comment. I thanked
you but asked "Why so reluctant?" —"Look at it," you
said, "You have not really looked." I had not, for all
my famed eagle-eye. The lady in red was a likeness of
you—swathed, all but smothered, in her bright tent of

clothes—beseeching time from her only companion, loyal, smiling, ready death. I said, "Never mind—just art not life" and you went off fishing.

Jessie, answer me this—if you saw yourself as the lady enthralled (danced buxom away), why did you hang it by your own front door, your last sight on leaving the house each day before heaving yourself into one more failure; and who did you see in the ashen young man, eyes down, in need of haircut, as he yields more slowly to his partner in the dance?

Never mind, again. All messages delivered. But till then at least, I work on here, issuing my own invitations (your message: *invitation unacceptable*)—house stocked with food (even crab, peach ice-cream), leaves broadening round me already, mid-April, a cave of green; pond boiling with fish now swollen with roe you could never catch though you tried countless hours; field cluttered with cows (your only phobia)—and when nights are sleepless and I slouch after work, facing my black window, the black woods beyond (the white-faced sniper we suspected there), the sight I want most often is you—a ghost in slacks!—to stretch by me here on my Navajo rugs (your bleak warning given and acted upon) and tell me the joke of the ape in love, so bad we could groan again in delight; and bare your heart (smooth, glistening now), face mine again (though younger, ruining).

Come at will, dear hulk, slimmed a little perhaps from your final fright but needless at last, free, no longer tired, and laughing to be homeless.

SUMMER GAMES

OUTSIDE, in our childhood summers—the war. The summers of 1939 to '45. I was six and finally twelve; and the war was three thousand miles to the right where London, Warsaw, Cologne crouched huge, immortal under nights of bombs or, farther, to the left where our men (among them three cousins of mine) crawled over dead friends from foxhole to foxhole towards Tokyo or, terribly, where there were children (our age, our size) starving, fleeing, trapped, stripped, abandoned.

Far off as it was, still we dreaded each waking hour that the war might arrive on us. A shot would ring in the midst of our play, freezing us in the knowledge that here at last were the first Storm Troopers till we thought and looked—Mrs. Hightower's Ford. And any plane passing overhead after dark seemed pregnant with black chutes ready to blossom. There were hints that war was nearer than it seemed—swastikaed subs off Hatteras or the German sailor's tattered corpse washed up at Virginia Beach with a Norfolk movie ticket in his pocket.

But of course we were safe. Our elders said that daily. Our deadly threats were polio, being hit by a car, drowning in pure chlorine if we swam after eating. No shot was fired for a hundred miles. (Fort Bragg—a hundred miles.) We had excess food to shame us at every meal, excess clothes to fling about us in the heat of play. So, secure, guilty, savage, we invoked war to us by games which were rites.

All our games ended desperately. Hiding, Prisoner's Base, Sling-Statue, Snake in Gutter, Giant Step, Kick the Can. We would start them all as friends, cool, gentle enough; but as we flung on under monstrous heat, sealed in sweat and dirt, hearts thudding, there would come a moment of pitch when someone would shout "Now *war!*" and it would be war—we separating, fleeing for cover, advancing in stealth on one another in terror, inflicting terror, mock death, surrender, till evening came and the hand of the day relaxed above us and cool rose from the grass and we sank drained into calm again, a last game of Hide in the dusk among bitter-smelling lightning bugs, ghost stories on the dark porch steps; then bath, bed, prayers for forgiveness and long life, sleep.

Only once did we draw real blood in our games; and I was the cause, the instrument at least. One August afternoon we had gone from, say, Tag into War. It was me, my cousins Marcia and Pat, and a Negro boy named Walter (who played with us for a quarter a week) against older, rougher boys. They massed on the opposite side of the creek that split the field behind our house. We had gathered magnolia seed pods for hand grenades; but as the charge began and swept toward us, as Madison Cranford leapt the creek and came screaming at me, he ceased being Madison (a preacher's son), the game ceased, the day rose in me, I dropped my fake grenade, stooped, blindly found a stone (pointed flint) and before retreating, flung it. My flight was halted by sudden silence behind me. I turned and by the creek on the ground in a huddle of boys was Madison, flat, still, eyes shut, blood streaming from the part in his sweaty hair, from a perfect circle in the skin which I had made. Walter, black and dry and powdered with dust, knelt by the head and the blood and looking through the day and the distance, said to me, "What ails you, boy? You have killed *this* child."

I had not, of course. He lived, never went to bed though a doctor did see him and pass on to us the warning that, young as we were, we were already deadly. My rock an inch farther down in Madison's temple would have done the work of a bullet—death. Death was ours to give, mine.

The warning was passed through my mother that night when she came from the Cranfords', having begged their pardon, and climbed to my room where I feigned sleep in a walnut bed under photographs of stars. I "woke" with a struggle, oaring myself from fake drowned depths, lay flat as she spread covers round me and heard her question launched, tense but gentle. "Why on earth did you throw a rock when everyone else was playing harmless?" What I suddenly knew I held back from her—that the others were not playing harmless, were as bent on ruin as I but were cowards, had only not yet been touched hard enough by hate. So I blamed the summer. "It was so hot I didn't know I *had* a rock. I was wild, for a minute. I will try not to do it again next summer." She said *"Ever* again" and left me to sleep which, tired as I was, did not come at once.

I lay in half dark (my sacred familiar objects crouched in horror from me against my walls) and thought through the lie I had told to save my mother —that summer was to blame. Then I said aloud as a promise (to my room, to myself), "I will tame *myself*. When the war is over and I am a man, it will all be peace, be cool. And when it is not, when summer comes, we will go to the water—my children and I— and play quiet games in the cool of the day. In the heat we will rest, separate on cots, not touching but smiling, watching the hair grow back on our legs."

Then sleep came unsought, untroubled to seal that further lie I had told to hide from myself what I knew even then—that I was not wrong to blame the summer, not wholly wrong; that wherever summer strikes (its scalding color), even in years of relative peace, something thrusts from the earth, presses from the air, compresses that in us which sets us wild against ourselves, in work, in games, in worst of all our love. Summer is the time wars live, thrive, on.

T H R E E

HOME LIFE

Truth and Lies

Good and Bad Dreams

A SIGN OF BLOOD

RAPID EYE MOVEMENTS

TWICE

WASHED FEET

SLEEPING AND WAKING

MORNING PLACES

TRUTH AND LIES

Guessing the signal Sarah Wilson flashed the car lights once. Nothing came or moved, only a rabbit close to the car, tan and quick in momentary light, eye congealed in terror. So she signaled again. Then dark and alone she said, "I will not break down. If she comes, if she's who I think she is, I will not give her that satisfaction." She shut her eyes to test her strength, to probe again the hole at the core of her chest. Then she hung her hands on the wheel, gripped till her ring ground loud on the grinding of crickets outside, and spoke again, "Don't let me break down now." That much was prayer to whatever might help —offered up through clear August night or ahead through glass to weeds of the railroad bank ten yards away where a girl had risen and stood now giant on the tracks and, seeing the second light, ran toward it. The crickets stopped as she split the weeds (safe down the bank from nights of practice), and her face stayed hid (a smile surely curled in the rims of her mouth). But she shrank as she came. That much made her bearable and when she crossed the last few feet and opened the door and lit the light, she reached her natural size; and Sarah Wilson could look and say, "Ella. I hoped it would not be you."

There had been no smile. There was none at their recognition. "Yes ma'm. It's Ella."

"And it's been you all this time."

Ella straightened into the dark, then leaned again. "I don't know how much time you mean, Mrs. Wilson."

"Oh I mean since before you were born, I guess."

"I am eighteen, Mrs. Wilson. It has been me since last December twentieth. Whoever was before me, I don't know her name."

That was true and saying it, hearing it, drained what was left of Ella's smile, Sarah Wilson's starting courage. So they hung in dull creamy light, picking each other's familiar faces for something to hate or forgive. But nothing was there, not yet, nothing they had not known and seen hundreds of times the past four years—Ella Scott's that had narrowed and paled beneath darkening hair to the sudden hot papery looks that all her sisters wore from the time they slouched through Sarah Wilson's class into a mill to watch loud machines make ladies' hose till the day they won boys who set them working on babies and the looks dried in as the skin drew yellow to their bones. And Sarah Wilson's that had never won praise even twenty years ago when she came here from college, had only won Nathan Wilson and then watched his life with no sign of cracking, yielding, except on her lips that did not close, that stretched back always to speak (speech being something that held back conclusions).

Sarah Wilson said, "I know. Sooner or later I know every name. But I didn't know yours till he came in at seven, drunk, and fell on the bed asleep and I undressed him and found this note." She took up a folded note from the seat, opened, studied it again—*I have got something to tell you and will be on the tracks tonight at eight o'clock.* No name. Then she looked to the girl. "Well, your writing has improved." Then "Ella, if you don't mean to run *now* and never come back, never see Mr. Wilson or me again, will you get in here and talk to me? You know I don't mean you harm."

"I know that, Mrs. Wilson." Ella still leaned in the open door, a hand on the seat-back. "I don't think I mean you no harm either; so if you need to talk—yes ma'm, I can listen."

Sarah Wilson's throat closed at that. Then she could say against her will, "I don't need anything you've got to give"; but she smoothed the cloth of the empty seat and Ella slid in. "Shut the door please. We have got to ride. We'll burn up here."

Ella nodded—ahead at the glass. "Yes ma'm. But I got to be home by ten o'clock. My daddy's home tonight and he wants me back."

"Whoever you're with?"

"Daddy knows who I'm with, who I come to meet anyhow."

"And he didn't stop you or warn you?"

"Mrs. Wilson, you know I have paid my way since I was sixteen." The engine ignited, the lights struck dust, weeds, the crest of the bank. "I have stood in that dimestore thousands of hours ringing up Negro quarters for some plastic nothing that lasts as far as the door. Daddy just owns the lock on the house—or rents it. He don't own me, if he ever did. Looks like nobody owns me now." She faced Sarah Wilson and managed a smile.

But Sarah Wilson missed it. She had taken the

wheel and turned them slowly toward the road; and
they went two miles in silence—flanking the tracks at
first and, beyond, the huddle of mill-owned huts where
Ella would sleep; then across on a road that narrowed
soon to a damp dirt swath through tobacco, cotton,
black pine. They did not look beyond open windows. It
was all their home, their daily lives. Ella stared forward.
Sarah Wilson drove and felt the questions stack in her
forehead; but the air swept cooler over them, bearing
the cold sound of crickets again, and when they had
passed a final house (its single light well back from the
road) and nothing lay ahead but eight miles of burnt
field, wild woods, Sarah Wilson started. "Ella, I think
you have told me the truth so far and I'm grateful; but
I'm asking you to answer some things I need to ask.
You may say it's none of my business—"

"—It's your business, yes ma'm. And I come on
this ride of my own will, so you got a right to ask
anything; but I got a right not to answer what hurts."

Sarah Wilson set that against what questions were
waiting, said to herself, "She is nothing but an ignorant
child Nathan tinkered with. I knew her, taught her
before she had power to hurt a flea much less break my
life. Don't let me hurt her now." She waited a minute
to strengthen that purpose. Then she started from the
edge. "You say it's been you since December twentieth.
That was the Christmas program."

"Yes ma'm. After Mr. Wilson carried you home,
he come back to check on us and close the auditorium.
Everybody was feeling good and it took awhile to clean
up the stage, and by then it had started sleeting. None
of the others were headed for the mill so Mr. Wilson
took me."

"—And started his Christmas drunk."

"No ma'm. Mr. Wilson don't drink where I am. I never have seen him take a drink. I have smelt it on him and known what it was—I have got brothers—but he has been nice about that with me."

"Well, he started it after he left you then and brought it to me next morning for Christmas. The drinking is something he saves for me."

"Yes ma'm. I noticed that was it. Marvin is that way—Aleen's husband. He'll be gone whole days at a time, but let him get tight and he heads for home and hands Aleen a drunk like his pay." It had come to her naturally—Aleen's trouble. But once it was out, she guessed it might slow Mrs. Wilson, win her a rest; so she faced the open window.

And it worked. Aleen was the first Scott girl, Ella's senior by nine or ten years. Once a student left Sarah Wilson's class, she lost count of dates, age, their work. But she often retained the thought of their faces. Years later they would rise when she saw in the paper their weddings, children, by now even deaths (faces full for that year with premature life knocking beneath still formless noses, jaws); and Aleen's came to her now as it had a month before when she read *Mrs. Marvin Maynard has returned to her home after two weeks in Baptist Hospital.* So slowing a little she said to Ella, "I saw Aleen was sick again. Same trouble?"

"Yes ma'm. Third time. They fixed her though so she couldn't go through it again—her heart's affected. This one lived four days but they said he wouldn't never be right. Then he died, which I guess was a blessing."

"Poor Aleen. Tell her I sent my sympathies to her."

"Yes ma'm. Aleen has not had a easy life. I

thought it would work this time. She took things easy,
wanted it so bad. To calm things down, she said."

The hole fell open in Sarah Wilson's chest. Her
foot weighed down on the gas; and she said, "You slept
with Mr. Wilson that first night, didn't you?"

"Yes ma'm."

"And you've gone on sleeping with him—eight
months nearly?"

"Yes ma'm, I have."

"And you don't think that's a sin?"

"Yes ma'm, I do."

"Then why didn't you stop? Just stop?"

"I don't know. Because Mr. Wilson was nice to
me, I guess. I don't mean to say he gave me things. He
didn't—oh a Pepsi now and then, and we drove twenty
miles for that so nobody wouldn't recognize him—but
he talked to me. He told me once he needed me to
listen. So I just listened."

"To what?"

"You know it already—the times he had when he
was a boy and being in the Army and coming here to
teach and jokes his classes play on him—"

"—And marrying me."

"No ma'm. He don't speak of you. The one time I
mentioned your name, he said 'Stop.' I was just saying
how good you had been when you were my teacher,
talking me into finishing high school and helping me
get that job."

"So you could hang around four more years to
sleep with my husband." She held back because they
had come to a junction, then stopped, thought, turned
to the left. Then, "Was he the first man you slept with,
Ella?"

The road they were on was paved again, concrete joints thudding under the wheels at a regular count of three; and shortly they met a car. Its light struck Ella's turned face and its horn tore loudly past them. Ella swung towards it and watched it away—four ducking heads, two laughing girls, two boys. Then facing backwards she started, flat and sudden, turning as she went, "I ain't *slept* anywhere near your husband. All him and me has had is a dozen or so twenty-minute spells on this dirty seat." She slung her thumb toward the dark back seat, looked to confirm the vacant place, rushed on—"No ma'm, he was not the first. He was just the nicest. Still is. He is the only person in my whole life who asks me what I want to do—and waits for me to decide. What we have done is what I wanted to do; and look what it's been so far"—her thumb stabbed again—"a lot of quick dirt. But I'm not turning loose. Not now. Not with the little I've got. No ma'm." Still half backwards she laid her head on the top of the seat, her eyes toward Sarah Wilson but shut, dry.

Sarah Wilson managed to drive through that; and when Ella finished they were on the outskirts of Kinley, Sarah Wilson's birthplace, hardly a town. She drove through it slowly, the car lights dully slapping two strips of wooden buildings that lined the road, three general stores, post office, gas pump; then, set back, the squatty houses that held what was left of the dozen white families who owned the stores, the farms, still owned the best part of whoever lived in the broken ring that lay in the dark, farther out behind this road (tenants, field hands, nurses, cooks). Beyond that far ring was Sarah Wilson's home, the place she dreaded. She was numb to the rest of Kinley; and she passed it thinking only, "I have gone too far. I will turn at the station and carry her home and ask her to quit."

The station was at the end of town. Only two trains a day came now, except for the freights that gathered pulpwood; and the evening train was surely gone, so the station should have been dark. But when she turned in, a last light showed in the passenger office, then vanished. She swung the car round on a cushion of pine bark; and just as she straightened to pull away, a man appeared in the station door and came down the steps, old and careful, not seeing till he reached the bottom. But then he waved and hurried toward them. It was Mr. Whitlow, the station master; and though he had been here always, Sarah Wilson had not seen him in the twenty-five years since he sold her the tickets that took her from Kinley to teacher's college. So she waited now and he came to Ella's side and said, "Train's left. Nothing on it but Negroes. Were you looking for somebody?"

Ella said "No" and looked to Sarah Wilson.

Sarah Wilson said, "It's Sarah Shaw, Mr. Whitlow —Sarah *Wilson*. I haven't seen you in twenty-five years."

He stared across and said, "Sarah Shaw. Has it been that long? Why don't you come to see us sometime?"

She said, "I keep busy. I do come down every once in a while to see Holt, but since Aunt Alice died I don't come much. She was the last I had down here."

He said, "I know it. I saw Holt today, walking past here. Straight as a rail and about as hard. Too mean to die. Is anybody out there with him now?"

"Not a soul and he says that's how he wants it. The others are gone—dead or in Richmond."

"Just Holt and the devil." He touched Ella's shoulder. "Sarah, is this your girl?"

"No sir. We don't have children. This is Ella Scott. She was my student four years ago."

"Was she a good one?"

"Good enough to finish. She finished this spring and is leaving for Raleigh, to business school."

He said "Good for her," looking past Ella to Sarah Wilson.

But Ella said, "I am thinking about it."

He studied her and said, "Go. If you've got good sense you'll get out of here. Your teacher yonder had the sense to leave. If she had stayed here she'd have died in misery twenty years ago. Trouble was, she came more than halfway back. *Love*, won't it, Sarah?"

"I don't remember that far. Maybe it was. How is your sister?"

He leaned farther in. "Sarah, I didn't mean you harm. Sister's alive—old like me. Not old enough to shut up though, not yet." He held his arm across Ella, his hand palm down; and Sarah Wilson took it a moment. "You did what you had to, Sarah. I hope you have got satisfaction in life. God knows you deserved it."

She thanked him and he withdrew his hand, touched Ella again and took four steps. Then before they moved he turned and said, "I never did ask could I help you tonight?"

Sarah Wilson said "No. Thank you, sir."

He said, "Well, I guess you know what you're looking for" and went across the road toward his home and his sister, using the beam of Sarah Wilson's lights as path.

She noticed that—that he walked in her lights—so

she waited and watched him, then realized the lights were dimmed and pressed with her foot to raise them; but he was gone, sooner than she'd counted on. She thought, "That is somebody else I will never see again"; and the new way was suddenly there—what to do, how to fight, maybe win, maybe save their lives. She looked to the clock, then to Ella. "We have got forty minutes. We might as well see this through."

Ella said, "I have said all I mean to say, Mrs. Wilson. Don't ask me no more questions tonight." She stared at her lap.

"I'm not. I'm not. What I know already will keep me sick long enough. But you say you have listened to Nathan so much. Now sit there and listen to me, to what you don't know, what Nathan wouldn't tell you if he talked ten years."

Ella stared on downwards, rocking the heel of one hand in her groin. She had said her say. Forty minutes was left and she could not walk eight miles tonight. She said, "I'm listening."

Beyond the station a dirt road cut back into the dark. It was one way—the old way—to Ogburn. It was also the way to Sarah Wilson's chance. She aimed them there and at once they were in total night, loud weeds pressing from the ditches, low pines choked with kudzu pressing above, boxing their lights. They sped through that till the sides opened out and the lights fell flat on fields of gapped dry corn that in nine hours would take the sucking sun again. The corn, the land were Holt Ferguson's, would be his for the next quarter-mile—and the dark oak grove, the house set back which they came to slowly on Ella's side. It was blacker than the sky behind it and so stood clear—a long low house hunched against the road.

Sarah Wilson stopped, not pulling to the edge, and leaned toward Ella to look. Then she drew back and made a small sign with her hand to the house. She hung that hand on the wheel and began, meaning it to be her life, the truth, that would speak for itself. "You can't see it now. There's no reason why you ever should; but when I was your age, I would sit in my room and press my head for relief, and what would come was the fact that I had this house, that if somebody would have *me*, we could come here and make as good a life as my parents had had. I thought this house was as surely mine as the soles of my feet. But I didn't even own the bed I was born in—a white iron bed behind that far big window on the right."

She pointed again, no hope of Ella seeing. "The house belonged to my father then—built for his marriage on land his father left—and that was their bedroom, his and my mother's. They slept there six years before I came. There was one boy before me who died, but I lived easily and I was the last. I never knew why. I used to ask Mother for brothers, company; and she would say, 'Sarah, I thought we were happy. Why aren't you satisfied?' I would think and decide I was. We were not rich—Father made eighty-five dollars a month as station agent plus half-shares on his farm—but we had what we needed, we valued each other, never stopped talking except from fatigue.

"Then when I was twelve they did try again on another child and that killed Mother. She lived four months after losing the child, but it poisoned her heart and she died one morning by the front porch swing. I had fallen at school and torn my skirt, and the teacher had sent me home to change. It was early November and warm, and she was out in the swing in her robe. Jane Phipps, her nurse, was sitting on the steps and Jane saw me first. I must have looked bad—dirty and torn—so Jane yelled, 'Sarah, what have you done?' and Mother stood up. I ran toward her to show I was safe, and she dropped at my feet. Thirty years ago and I know every second, could draw it if I could draw. Nobody told me. I saw it.

"I saw the next three years too, but I barely remember them. They were the happiest—after the shock, when Father and I were here alone. I've thought about that—not remembering those years—and I know it's *because* we were happy. I have never forgotten one painful thing. So we had three years. I say *we*. I was happy and I thought Father was. I thought we were sufficient to one another and would go on being; but when I was fifteen one June morning, I was sweeping the yard and a Negro boy ran up and said, 'Yonder—they are rolling your father home.' I ran for the road and met them on that last curve. They had him on a two-wheeled mail cart—black Ben Mitchell and Mr. Whitlow who was Father's help. They stopped when they saw me, and Ben waited in the shafts while I looked. Father couldn't speak. He had had a stroke, forty-eight years old.

"It didn't kill him, not more than half. But that was when Holt saw his chance—Holt Ferguson, Aunt Alice's husband. She was Father's half-sister—his mother's child older than him—so the Shaw land was Father's; and he let it out on halves to tenants. Well, when Father could sit up and halfway talk, Holt came and said he and Alice would move here and keep house and

farm as long as they could be of service. I was in the
room. Father thought ten seconds; then he turned to
me and said 'Sarah, how about it?' It killed me to think
he would welcome them when we had done so well
alone; so I said the house and land were his, that he
could ask in gypsies or Negroes, that I would be gone in
two more years. He caught at his breath but he managed to tell me to calm myself; then he turned to Holt
and said, 'Come ahead. We need you. I thank you and
so will Sarah when she understands.'

"But I never understood—only that the Fergusons
came and went to work, on the farm and on Father;
and from that day I recall every waking minute till
now. I have slept very little. Father and I had the right
side of the house, but we crept around and cleaned up
after ourselves like cats. So did Holt and Aunt Alice—I
give them that. She never did an unkind deed in her
life, and Holt was working till late most nights. It was
the boys I minded. They were younger than me and
the house was their home in fifteen minutes, every rock
in the yard. I grieved myself to sleep every night, but I
never spoke another word to Father about asking them
here. I got through the worst by telling myself, 'This
place is Father's and will someday be mine.' And when
Father was working—he limped around part-time—I
fought for my own, thinking I knew what was my
own.

"But I didn't, not till Father died. He lived till I
was seventeen. Then the second stroke came and took
him at the station on the *floor*, with no time to tell me
what he had done. What I knew was what Aunt Alice
told me after the funeral—that no plans were changed,
that Father had arranged it with Holt, I was going to

college and should think of this as home. So I lived
through that last summer, sleeping in the bed I was
born in, thinking I would go and come back and teach
and marry—I was not in love; I had friends but no one
I needed—and give the Fergusons the old Shaw place
and start my life. September came and Tim, Holt's
oldest boy, drove me to the station. I bought a roundtrip ticket from Mr. Whitlow; and when we could hear
the train in the rails, I said to Tim, 'I will see you
Christmas.' He said, 'I'll meet you. You might not
know the house.' I said 'Why?' and he said, 'After we
put on that new kitchen.' I said it was odd that Holt
hadn't told me; and over the whistling train Tim said,
'I guess since it's his, he didn't think to tell you.' That
was the first I knew, first *hint*. There was nothing to do
but ride the train and wait for a letter.

"It came a week later—from Aunt Alice begging
my pardon, saying Holt and the boys thought I knew,
that she was supposed to tell me but failed. Father had
sold Holt everything. He had seen he was dying, he
must have remembered me saying those things, and he
saw only one way to get me to college. Holt had got it
—house and land—for the price of college and his
word to give me a home if I needed one. I didn't then.
I redeemed what was left of that roundtrip ticket.
Then I went four years without seeing Kinley. In the
summers I stayed at school and worked to pay for my
clothes. I make it sound bad. It did seem the worst of
all my luck, but once I got breath I was not that
unhappy. God knows I wasn't happy, but I had work to
do and friends to visit in my few vacations. One was
Martha Hawkins in Ogburn.

"I went to her on Christmas night of my last year

in college. I had spent three days in Kinley, here. Aunt Alice asked me, saying I had broken her heart, so I came. I had had four years to show my feelings and I made up my mind to do my share of healing wounds. So had they. We grinned through a lot of food and presents, and she put me in Mother and Father's room; but I thanked God hourly that I had arranged to leave Christmas day for Martha's. When I left, Aunt Alice said they hoped I would come here to live and teach. I thanked her and said I would take the best offer wherever that was. Then again Tim drove me away, to Ogburn. That time he hardly spoke so I rode alone with what I had after those three days, twenty-one *years*—a suitcase of clothes, three Christmas gifts, three-fourths of a college diploma. Not one other thing and I knew it.

"Well, I took the first offer, not the best. It came from Nathan Wilson. Martha was giving a party that night; and when I walked in, he was the first thing I saw—Nathan—and within an hour I was telling him this same story. *Because he was drunk.* I don't make a policy of sharing trouble; but drunk as he was, he read my face and when we were half alone, he said, 'Who knocked the props from under you?' and I told him, whispering so no other human would hear. He said, 'She was right. You must come here and live and make peace or you'll die on the run.' I had seen from the first that he was running—drunk two states north of his home—but I asked him what he was running from and he told me. Himself of course and what he had done to people that loved him—his dead mother and the first girl that offered him her life. But you know all that if you've listened like you say. I listened then—listen now

130

if he asks me to—and when we were done, I had offered him my life too. Not that night, not openly, though before I slept I could feel he had stuck himself in my mind like a nail, being like me—running from wrecks, needing someone to halt him, plug up his chest.

"The next afternoon he came back to Martha's and begged my pardon for anything out of the way he had done—*out of the way* when he was already what I needed. We took a ride that afternoon and he said there was something he *had* meant—that I must come here to teach—and he offered me a job. He had come to Ogburn as principal three years before. Being what he was, he made me think he was right; and I accepted, already back in my mind, making peace. Then he drove me to Kinley to tell Aunt Alice. She said to Nathan, 'If you are the reason, I am grateful to you.' I laughed but he *was* and I was so grateful I married him. He had come to see me most weekends; and by May when he asked me, I knew everything I would ever know—that his past was people he had let down and left—but I needed him and I thought he needed me. He never said so but he acted like need, still does—coming to me tonight like a child, not even trying to hide your note. So I said Yes, eyes open, and we married in June, here.

"Holt gave me away which was not easy, but we said it was part of our new beginning. *Beginning* when in two years it had died on my hands—Aunt Alice dead and Holt alone going harder and harder; Nathan and I crammed in rooms in Ogburn teaching all week, then taking long dark Saturday rides to buy his liquor, watching him pour it down secret from everyone but

me, watching him tear on past me in this race I can't
stop, can't slow, taking the best part of me with him
through his hot quick dirt as you call it. But not killing
it—the need I have to gouge out the drinking and
women and calm him. The women anyhow. They
started six years after our marriage when we finally
knew we could not have children. It wasn't me that
wanted them—things going so badly—but during those
years I would sometimes say, 'Nathan, when will you
stop?' and he would say, 'When I have a child to hide
from.' He had never had to hide a thing from me.
Then we found it was him at fault. There was one
more hole through the middle of him. He was really
no *good*—"

Ella said "Stop." She had heard every word looking down, not moving, giving Sarah Wilson that
chance; but she pointed now to the lighted clock—the
dim lights were on. "I have got twenty minutes. What
are you trying to tell me please?" Then she faced Sarah
Wilson.

It took her awhile to know. "I have just now told
you. Nathan Wilson is no good to you, no good on
earth to anyone but me. What do you want out of half
a man, young as you are?—when the half has been
mine twenty-one years, is grown to me and must never
tear loose. *Will* not."

"I was not *tearing* nothing—I wish I had been. I
do not love your pitiful husband. What I said tonight
—about not turning loose—I said it wild. You made
me say it, digging so ugly. Mr. Wilson is yours and I
thank God for it. But I need to see him one more
time."

"No Ella, please. Just end it now."

"You are too late, Mrs. Wilson. Two days too late. I have turned loose already, *torn* loose. I have ended the little we had, myself." She took up the note from the seat beside her, held it between them. "But I told him here I had something to say."

"Then say it to me. I'll see that he knows."

"He knows, he knows. Oh—" Ella shut her eyes, clamped her teeth, said, "Say to Nathan, to Mr. Wilson, that Ella has done what she promised to—" Breath and force refused, sucked back into her, grated her throat. Her hand wadded in on the note; her head faced the black grove, the house. Then noise came in chunks from the pit of her neck.

That saved Sarah Wilson, gave her strength to crank the car, turn it, aim for Kinley, the highway, the quick way to Ogburn—thinking she had won and numb from winning, from not breaking down. Past Kinley she steered on quickly through fields darker now, insects thicker and dazed by the heat, no other car in sight and only one man in the eight fast miles—a Negro stalled, beside his old truck in open white shirt, one hand on a fender, the other flapped once like a wing as they passed, signing for help he did not expect (as if she could help an angel of light after this night's work, could speak again, even think, before morning). Yet they were nearly back and soon she would have to speak—whatever awful last thing to Ella, to calm her, thank her, find the end of her message to Nathan. Sarah Wilson slowed to plan her speech but too late— her lights had nudged the first ranks of mill huts coiled so dense they would flash in a trail if one spark dropped, dark in the windows but each throwing naked hall-light into dwarf dirt yards through open doors. She

checked the time. Five more minutes and Ella's father
would wait in one door, ready to lock. Not wanting to
know which house was Ella's, she took the tracks; and
when Ella looked up puzzled, she said, "I will put you
out where I met you—here." They were there again at
the foot of the bank and Sarah Wilson stopped.

Before they were still Ella reached for the door.

Sarah Wilson touched her, her cool bare arm.
That was the thanks. Then she said, "Ella, wait. I did
not mean to press you to tears. What I meant to do
was tell you my life and let that speak as a warning to
you. But I went too far, telling that secret. That is *our*
grief, mine and Nathan's. I had no right to give it to
you. I beg your pardon and, bad as what you have done
may be, I thank you for promising to leave him now.
I'll hold you to it. So give me your message and go on
home where your father is."

Ella opened the door, slid from beneath Sarah
Wilson's hand, then leaning in as she had at the first—
but her hair caved down on her bloated eyes—she said
clearly, "I have not promised you nothing, Mrs. Wilson. I won't need to see your husband again, but that's
not because of a promise to you or because of what you
thought up tonight. The promise I made was to Nathan Wilson; and I went to Raleigh this week and kept
it—went on the *bus* and ditched a baby in a nigger
kitchen for two hundred dollars. Tell him that and tell
him I said I will pay him back my half when I can
work." She said that three feet from Sarah Wilson's
face. Then she turned and walked toward the tracks,
leaving the car door open. She went slowly purposely to
show she was free; that whatever her debts, she owned
herself.

Yet slow as she was, she reached weeds and bank before her meaning reached Sarah Wilson's mind, entered through still open mouth, spread through palate, skull. Her head had turned forward while Ella spoke; and it stayed there rigid, seeing Ella walk, then quicken in the weeds and take the bank running, stumbling on top to her hands and knees but rising at once, sinking on the far side slowly again. Sarah Wilson shut her eyes, struggled to shut her mouth; but it hung apart— taut not slack as if it would speak of its own will, free and pure. Yet no words came, only the strength to move the car, give it signals to take her home—at least to where Nathan slept (if he slept, if he was not gone), breathing aloud on the bed they shared.

The car obeyed and turned beneath her toward Ogburn. There would be one mile of air to breathe before the town streets exhaling day, the houses she knew, that knew her, knew all but this night and would soon know this—if it was true, had been and would last beyond morning. That hope, simply, sent her on—that it *all* was lie, would end when Nathan woke and eased her. But the car reached Ogburn. It did not slow. It mounted the hump where paving began and threw light left on the first open yard, scalding a rabbit with sudden discovery. Tan and quick it was sucked toward Sarah Wilson, beneath her wheel. In the bones of her hand—her fine bones gripped to swerve—she felt its brittle death. Too late she braked, slewed in the street, halted. Then her mouth spoke freely its waiting threat. "How could I, why should I tell the truth when I thought I could save what was left of our life—that had *stopped*." Her lips sealed down. Grunts like steam rammed her heart, her teeth.

GOOD AND BAD DREAMS

1. A *Sign of Blood*

She went out at eight, leaving him asleep. So he let her believe. He was only waiting behind shut eyes to have the room still and empty at last, his for the day—his first free solitary day in months; *years* it felt, by the weight that dissolved with each breath now. As he flung back the covers and stood, he thought "Chance." The word itself, clearly. Then, stripped and shuddering (she had not lit the heater), he smiled— chance for what? Well, nine free hours. The room his again. But *warm* first.

He scissored to the heater in three steps, squatted, inhaled, threw the gas jet. The breath was one that he always took—shallow and secret—before lighting the gas (fear of breathing fire; she had never noticed). But alone now, he also flinched at the puff. A minor luxury —with her he could not show a hint of fear.

Waiting in the warmth, he rocked farther forward to see the room upside down through his crotch. His dangling sex transfixed the unmade bed—stake in the heart of the vampire at the crossroads! He actually laughed, and caught the frail permanent scent of his groin—the room's ground-bass. He made, for the first time since adolescence, the lunge to kiss his sex. It needed the notice. But he fell on his tail and lay in the laughter like warming water.

A mirror. A long pierglass hung beside him. Flat on his back, he could not see himself—only windows opposite, still covered against light. So he stood, square before it, no longer smiling, chin firm and lifting, clenched hands at his sides—an archaic Apollo: *You must change your life*—even strode one solemn step forward toward his image. Unmoving, he studied his image by gaslight. The chest broad but flat (a pale hard tray); arms, legs thin and long, joint flowing easily into bone without display. "I am lovable," he said and kissed on the mirror all the mirror would permit—his lips. They could use the greeting at least. Then he went to the window to open the curtains.

Light. His day. He could open them safely, naked as he was, since the room faced backward, the high thick garden, no other house there. Only at the sight did he think of the storm. In the night he had waked to hear wind and rain; she had spoken—what? a word about the roof; would it hold through this? he had said "Live in hope" and fallen off again.

The roof had clearly held. The yard showed torn limbs and leaves but no shingles. He could work on that awhile, clearing trash—the day was not bright but neither was it freezing. No, he would read, draw, listen to music. First, to bathe and dress. The garden could wait. Let the trash be compost.

But, turning from the window, his eye snagged at one dark spot in the ground—a cap? a glove? Something soaked and wadded on bare dirt by the door. Tan or gray? He strained to see which, and consciously wondered *why?*—why linger on this? He was twenty yards away and above it; and he stared till he knew it was tan—or a richer brown, russet. Fur. A drowned mole?—it was larger than a mouse. He could not find limbs or eyes in its mass. Whatever, it was still. Dead. More rubbish.

Yet when he had turned and moved toward the bath, he felt the day begin to leak from his grip, like all the others. He knew what sapped them, every day for years—his promise to her—but this threat was new, with a taste of its own, a dry density. Oh a nag, not a threat. He stopped by the bed, still yards from the bath, and smelled himself. He was clean enough.

He was back at the window. The small corpse was there, still resisting knowledge, crouched on its precious death. Or was it only a scrap of a corpse?—rabbit, squirrel fur? No sign of blood, not from here at least.

He dressed in two minutes, was down and standing directly above it, and still did not know. He knelt and bent till his face was no more than a foot away. Lice, in the fur. They had ridden out the storm and were still hustling blood that was jelly by now. Then he noticed wings—the hooked tips of leather wings intricately folded. A bat.

Of course he stood. He had never seen a bat. Maybe in a zoo or occasionally swooping round a distant street lamp. But never this close. *Unprotected.* He felt instantly stripped again and vulnerable, precisely in his eyes and throat. He blinked and stepped back but knew it was dead and forced his fear down. He must move it though. How? Nudge it along with his foot toward the trashpile. Rabies—no. There had been rabid bats—two, three summers ago. Children had been bit. These lice were alive and stuffed with its blood. He must bury it deeper than dogs could smell.

When he found the shovel, he returned and stood again. Its back seemed shrunk, as though essence were leeching into dirt already. It was toy-sized, a winged mouse whacked down by wind. He would bury it in soft ground beyond the garbage. He slid the spade toward it gently—a funeral!—neatly, respectfully under it.

It convulsed—flung itself to its back on the spade, stretched its wings full-out, bared baby-pink gums, white needle teeth and—surely—screamed.

He knew it would rush at his face—his eyes—and he dropped the shovel to run; ran three steps. Then he stopped to see, remembering her—as though she were there in the window above him, his panic slamming at her.

Already it was calming—had flopped again to its belly on the ground and was folding its joints slowly inward again.

He knew it was dying, maybe of rabies; and though he had read of explorers infected with rabies by drizzling bat piss in caves, he knew he was safe so far—his skin unbroken, dry. Let it die there in its own good time, where it chose to fall, arranged as it wished. Only the shovel, abandoned beside it, disordered the scene. That could also wait. He turned to the house again, his day recovered. It was only eight-thirty; only this square yard of ground was off-limits. The other world was his.

*   *   *

Yet an hour later—fed, bathed, shaved, dressed
again—he could do nothing more than stand at the
window and watch the bat. It was still condensed too
tautly for death. However it perceived its struggle, it
struggled. "So would any virus"—he mocked his own
thoughts as the bat threw them up. Why is a bat, the
size of your hand, a source of terror when a horse, say,
is not or even a frog? Childhood icons?—Halloween,
vampires? Or older even, archetypal?—built into our
genes since cave men fought them back with brands? A
brush of wet fur across the lips in sleep, leather-coated
struts of bone clasped to baby's throat?

When he'd dealt with all the clichés, he was left
with its win. It had hogged his day—or two hours of his
morning. If for no older reasons, then, an enemy. Kill
and bury it. Broadside with the shovel. It must anyhow
be gone when she returned.

Why? Why could she not be trusted, at her age,
with the entire equipment of the created world? Why
fence off this or that? Let her grow her own rind or
shrink from sight. God knew he'd grown *his*.

So he went for himself. Slowly, sanely down again.
"My race has agreed to hold bats repulsive. I'm man
enough then to object to a sick bat dying in the yard."
That served as reason through the quick kill and bury-
ing. It had been nearly gone—no more Dracula feints,
just a quick relaxing as the spade slapped once. It had
even had the grace not to bleed a drop. A tidy bat.

He buried it whole, on its belly as it chose—like
everything dead, two sizes smaller; ludicrously defused
—and not till he'd climbed to the room again, lighter,
having won, and had bent to make their bed (the

sheets as unused as invalids') did he know why the
thing had destroyed his day and demanded brutality
and—four ounces of leather, lice, fur—would change
his life (something he and Apollo had never managed). It was messenger, sign.

No. Absurd. From whom? And how cheap—the
celestial joker's usual taste.

She will kill herself.

2. *Rapid Eye Movements*

But who believes signs? Who can know what he knows till his knowledge is useless, beached by event? In a day, he'd forgot his sense of omen; and the afternoon of the second day (a Sunday, both at home), he was on her again, employing her facilities—or the single one he needed, in the late clear light.

She permitted him. He also knew that, but would not think of it—that she endured his poking in silent still puzzlement, as though he belonged to another species with analogous parts but incomprehensible needs or as though she were a faith (and the faith's central shrine) and he were the priest of a heresy who entered to perform his rite on her altar—in her presence and hearing but in language and gesture and, finally, reward that were sealed from her.

He'd have thought it out in some such language— and been eased by the image—if she'd given him time. But once he'd finished and paused for breath, he started again, entirely for her, slow deep strokes to offer her the coup.

She did not say Yes or No, her hands still lay— neither urgent nor repelled—in the small of his back. She only breathed deeply at the pit of each stroke—her breaths rock-steady, no quickening.

He slowed and raised to see her face.

Her eyes were shut; the muscles of her mouth and throat were still. She was nearly asleep.

"Later?" he asked. He thought she nodded; her

chin dipped once. He rolled gently off her. Her body
adhered for a half-turn toward him; so he lay and
watched her slide into sleep, intending to think his way
out now, her sighing head an aid to contemplation.

She gave him ten seconds to think of her warmth
—in the room where he was rapidly cooling, she sent a
firm heat across the gap between them (they were not
touching, ten inches apart)—then her eyes began to
move. Behind the thin lids, a quick frail jittering at
first.

Rapid Eye Movements. The sign of a dream. He
moved his own face closer to hers, slowly, not to wake
her; and strained to see the story she saw. Soon the
random movements slowed a little and settled into
steadier horizontal sweeps—the balls of both eyes rolling left and then right, as though following a lazy
tennis game. Then the slow sweeps would be broken by
lurches—upwards or sideways. Then tennis again.

Or her battling parents. Yes. She had told him an
hour before—the first time—of a night in her childhood out of Dickens or Zola—her father drunk and
beating her mother. Her mother would run to a corner,
crouch for more; her father would follow; and she, age
five, had waked and come and flown between them, a
shuttlecock, screaming for quiet. Surely that was what
her shut eyes saw now. And would see till he stopped
her. The circular past, she its willing victim. He called
her name twice.

She shook; her eyes opened. She did not smile. "I
was dreaming," she said.

"I know," he said and laid a hand on her, below
her right breast.

*   *   *

What he does not know, what she will not tell him, is that her dream was not of her parents but plainly of themselves, not past but future—her need to stop their life. Need and plan. To wake her is not to end it.

3. *Twice*

Sʜᴇ is still right-handed. She holds the razor-blade —new, firm, single-edged—with that calm hand and extends the left arm.

The white, blue-strung antecubital space; the bend of that arm. She cuts with the chicken-flesh grain at the bend, three-quarters of an inch deep, two inches long. Her hand has not paused, the line is straight. The brachial artery and vein lurch, astonished; then pump on, but now in the air of the room. The arm clasps to her side. She has planned in advance to rush her death by assisting the artery—clenching and opening her left hand in rhythm. What she has not known is that, choosing this spot, she has cut (no choice) the median nerve. Her left hand and wrist are paralyzed. Useless, though wet. Her left thigh and calf, left foot, are wet; the white tile cubes of the floor are wet over eighty square inches.

Yet she still feels *herself*. She is still herself—what she's been all her life, less this much blood. Continuity.

She cuts again, as slowly and deeply, an inch above the previous cut, in clear flesh. The line is straight again. She severs the same vein, artery, nerve and tendons a second time. There is still pain enough to shake a house. "Supererogation"—she thinks that and smiles.

4. Washed Feet

HE HAS slept this soundly since four in the morning because when he came back, his mind was clear. It
knew only one thing—the doctor's words on leaving
her ward, "She can live if she wants; we've done that
much." (They had, the doctor and his nameless team,
had worked four hours repairing her try, patiently ligat-
ing all she'd severed—the brachial artery and vein—
anastomosing tendons, pumping in the mandatory
blood that would be at least no stranger to her than the
pints she'd carefully drained tonight; then had wheeled
her still unconscious to a lighted ward and watched her
like a bomb.) The words had instantly swelled in his
head, a polished plug molded to crowd his skull and
exclude all else, every atom of air. And had perfectly
succeeded. He had come here—a half-hour walk, a taxi
—had lit the gas-fire (no other light), then stripped and
slept. No question of why or who was at fault—"The
woman with whom I have lived six years has tried to
kill herself. A serious try—no skittish theatrics. I found
her; they saved her; she can live if she wants." No question of how.

Two hours of dreamless sleep. It is six, but still
winter dark; only the low red burn of the gas—he is
sleeping his own way, in warmth.
This happens. A man is in the room, standing
darkly in a corner. In his sleep, he sees the man and

does not feel fear or curiosity; only watches till he knows what's required of him—that he thrust with his bare feet till they've cleared sheets and blankets and lie exposed. That is the necessary sign. The man moves forward to the end of the bed; stands waiting, still dark. No question of seeing his face or dress. He is dark. No need to know—only lie there flat on your back and wait. Now the man is looking round the room—he is needing something. Lie still, he will find it. And the man goes on looking, even moves a few steps in various directions. Is his face distraught?—lie still, don't wonder, he can fill his own needs. In calm desperation, the man returns to his place at the end of the bed; kneels suddenly. He silently spits in the palms of both hands and washes the bare feet propped before him. The gestures are gentle but the palms are rough.

He is scrubbed awake. He lies on his back, his feet are uncovered, they sweat though the room is hardly warm. He raises his head to see the room. Empty of all but red gas light and the customary stuffing, their stifling freight. He knows he was dreaming. No man is here. No one but himself.

Yet he also knows (he falls back for this) another new thing, more filling than the last—that from now (this night, this momentary dream) he must walk in his life as though a man had been here—one who had come precisely here by choice and, desperate to forgive, had searched for water, then knelt and washed his feet (till then unjudged) with the agent available—His spit, that wishes to clean but scalds.

5. Sleeping and Waking

AT THE end of his dream he fell or flew. Fall or flight, free or pursued, he could not say which, only that he hurtled or was sucked through space; but in his dream he knew he must know (as he must know awake), and he questioned his sleeping body. The legs, arms, head of his dream were calm; and his heart stroked on calm of fear or dread (his actual heart, the heart in his dream), flushing through him the news that he would be spared, that he would rush on, then a cord would rein him, arms or nets stretch to bear him, stop him in time. And he was stopped at last but not by arms, by one word said in an unknown voice—"Lucas" his name—trapped in terror, the voice a mouth on his helpless chest, dull-toothed, draining. He must wake or die and, asleep, he began to flail—at first with his will, then with actual arms against hot dark till he woke on his numb left side, in bed, his right hand fallen on her hip he had struck, in what light there was.

It was night, would be night for hours (he sensed it through blinds, saw it above in the well of the ceiling); but the room was red from the low gas fire that had burned on beside their sleep—another threat that had spared them, done only the duties of fire. The air was stifling and both their bodies though dim were clear. That had been her purpose. When they had stripped and were ready, she had said, "Let it burn. I can see you plainly." But sleep after eight weeks smothered his force, and soon they had turned into separate chaos. Now he saw. Maybe this was her purpose—not the sight of love but that he see her, separately drowned, raw to whatever might strike or seize.

So he saw—knowing he was safe, knowing from her breath, her tamed smell, that she slept, that his dream was his own, his hand unfelt. She slept on her right side toward him, and up from his hand she was mainly dark for the fire was beyond her. Only the crest of her side was lit—jack-knifed legs, the hip he pressed, sunken waist, the left arm splayed behind her—but he forced his eyes to her face. Then from six years' memory he remade it slowly—in stiff black hair a white heart of skin (smooth still but taut) cut by tiers of what now seemed wings—her upward brows, shut eyes, lashes (all wings to leave), a long top lip crouched even in sleep like the edge of an unstitched wound, a full bottom lip almost Negro brown, color of the first real scar beneath in the boneless pit of her neck where twenty years before in child's pneumonia a silver pipe had saved her life, color of the rounds of her breasts raised now, stretched by the backward cast of her arm, lighter only in color than all her hair, than her folded center a hand's breadth below his hand.

His eyes stopped there. For a while it seemed a resting place—dark core of a dark room, harbor, home, socket of his life. From which his life was wrenched eight weeks before, by her, for her own blind reasons which she had not told, would not, maybe could not.

The question was why? and he did not know, had still after eight weeks failed to ask, not knowing whether he had the right, whether six years gave him the final right to save her life, fight off the death she had tried to choose, might choose again when she woke. But she slept on beside him, beneath his hand; and seeing, he thought of sleepwalkers, oracles—answerers. And because he was free in this brief safety, he said to himself that if she would sleep, lie dim and drowned, he would rise to her ear and ask for her reasons, ask who was innocent? guilty? why?—force her answer, know before she woke.

She moved. Before he could ask or smile at himself, she turned away, crushing her left arm beneath her, sliding dry beneath his hand till she stopped nearly flat, his hand on her core. He let it rest, straining with eyes—jaws, even—to hold it calm, not to move or demand what time after time he had silently demanded, got. Then she seemed to flicker in that one place as animals choose one muscle from thousands to twitch beneath a fly—or a wanted hand. He thought she had waked, was conscious and waiting for his demand, demanding his need.

He would not, not demand, not ask for this so simply offered when he could not ask for his desperate need—her reasons, the blame. He took his hand to his own hard flank which, shielded by her, was colder—but was his, to count on. And free from his weight, she moved again, flatter, face to the ceiling, eyes and lips shut. He saw that—her face—heard her doubtful breath begin again. She had not waked. So he raised himself on his elbow above her, lowered his face till her frail breath touched him.

She frowned—the way his mother had frowned at the rise of death, from her belly a wave of dead blood flung blue toward her throat, thrusting chin, locked teeth, pressed eyes. Helpless, he only watched it rise,

take not only her face but whatever mind worked on
under sleep, telling himself it would leave as it came.
But it held her, her face a mask, mirror—simply—of
the only death he had watched, his mother's. Yet it was
a mask, not death itself. Her lungs sighed on. He must
wake her though, spare her this ordeal whatever it was.
He could do that—but slowly, gently. He laid his face
to her breast and, rocking his jaw, kneaded the flesh
above her heart, the shielding bones, with the stumps
of his beard—and forced a word, one sound, from her
dream. It was a dream. He knew that now and whatever her dread, old or new, he would let her bear it,
riding above her, one ear to her heart, one cocked for
another word, her answer. "Whatever she says, if she
speaks again, let it be the answer." He said that clearly
though silently. "I will take what she says as her reason,
her blame, and use it to save her, if she will speak."

She said his name—"Lucas"—aloud but in nothing like her daily voice, in the voice that had come at
the end of his dream to break his fall.

He could break hers—and would. The question
was why? but the answer was who. She had answered
"Lucas" which gave him the blame but also the right
and duty to save her. He rose from her chest to his
knees above her, turned to face her, straddled her body
at the parted calves, then bent, extended her hid left
arm and kissed the two scars parallel as rails where she
had slashed her veins eight weeks before. He felt her
waking rise beneath his lips. For the final moment in
all his life, he was safe, alone, free. Now he must look,
take her open eyes (her answer his secret)—must and
would. Then he could start his pitiful humping
amends.

6. Morning Places

A⊤ FOUR in the morning, having ceased to hope, he flings himself onto shallow sleep, random beside her— no rest but a flailing, oaring dumbness that leads him in terror, total dark, to the pitch of abyss where he wakes, fingers clawed against fall, heart seized. But attentive, attending, in every pore, straining to name this room, bed, woman beside him Her slow breath crosses the air between them, chills his side but places him—"Home, our bed, my wife beside me." Saying that seems a form of stripped prayer, the core of surren- der, "Your will. Yours." Then sleep is allowed him. He falls back from her and sinks for an hour, thoughtless, mute, gladly drowned. Then at five—the room still black, no sign of day—he bares this dream to himself in his clear mind's voice as carefully, slowly, as if it were new, were made this moment at whosever will to strengthen his rest, were never true.

"I lie asleep in my home, our bed, my place beside her—her at my left eight inches away but separate from me in all her length. I lie on my back as now, eyes shut; yet I have other eyes that lift through dark and witness from above, with no wish, will, fear or strength. So I see her waken, her eyes click open, all pupil for the dark but also fearless—yet willing and strong and look- ing only up, not to my still body. Her first move is speech. Her lips make five words but I cannot hear, only witness her readiness. She gathers her arms

(winged above her head), her scattered legs—touching
me no more than if I were fire—sliding left from me
and, to spare me, rises as though she were weightless,
jarring nothing as she goes—white gown, bare feet, bare
arms, hands at her sides, fingers calmly spread. Past our
door, she has left my actual body—all that might have
saved her—but the eyes of my dream are allowed to
stand in that door and watch her go twelve counted
steps, stop, raise her hand to a light, a mirror—I see her
ready face and cannot move, do not wish to act—a
cabinet, a blade. Then that blade lowered to the bend
of her left arm—bare, no bone between her life and
her. She opens a line and before the astonished blood
can start, opens a second, parallel above it as though it
were ruled. She stretches the arm at her side, pumps
her fist. Her feet, the floor are wet with her life. Then
she turns toward me—the eyes of my dream, my hidden body—and takes the first steps, her arm now
bowed at her chest, blood blooming suddenly as if from
her breasts, heart, belly, core; red blade still in her red
right hand. I see that and only count her nearing steps.
On the fifth she begins to become something new—on
her face at first which is not the face she carried away
nor the face we have made in these six years but her
early face and for two steps armed with that face like a
sword. Then she bears a sword. The blade enlarges
upward in her hand, its blood now fire—all her blood
streaming fire, her arms sucked up into metalled wings,
feet shod, heart shielded, riveted, only her early face
unchanged. Having only eyes, I cannot fear; but at her
last steps, I lose those eyes and am only my sleeping
self in dark till I wake on my back in scalding heat.
Stood above me, straddled my knees, scalding my face,

bare chest, covered heart, is what she became in the last
few steps, what I have known since a child as an angel
and—by its face no longer hers, neither man nor woman's, its black eyes steady discs through the heat, its red
mouth sealed to question or plea—a final angel, judge
and killer. Yet its sword is upward, clamped in gloved
fists; and its eyes though set are not on me but over my
head, beyond through paper, plaster, lathing, stone. By
that I am strengthened to ask its will. I say 'What is
your name?' No answer, waver, flicker of notice. I say,
'Am I the man you have come to find?' It moves at
that, forward both legs till between its ankles it presses
my unguarded flanks. 'Why have you come here?' and
knowing its mission, still, 'What do you need from
me?' Its lips have vanished. Beneath its nose it is
smooth to the chin. 'Take what you need.' I lie fully
back, lift my chin to bare my throat, extend the tender
pit of my arm. And it takes my offer, bows to its need.
Its fists untwine, the sword of its own weight sinks
toward me. These eyes are blinded but I wait for its
stroke, lips sealed against cry. It is on my mouth—the
stroke—and my lips part behind it like edges of a
wound; but what I issue is speech not blood, one word
'Pardon' as the sword lifts. The stroke has forced me to
say it once and, sparing me, compelled me to say it
always—'Pardon,' that flatly, both plea and gift. My
blindness continues but the heat recedes; and then I
am seeing again—the ceiling. Still flat, I jerk my eyes
round the room. There in the far corner, cooling and
clearing, stands she again, her simple self, a younger
she, unarmed, clothed in her early beauty (sword
enough) yet bleeding in reach now and beckoning to me
with her whole wrecked arm. Her force sucks at me like

a need to fall. I lurch to rise, to rush to save her; but my heart refuses, inhales its blood, jells it within me. I may not go, not save her life; but with all my force I reach my knees, free my voice, tell her 'Pardon,' saying to myself, 'I must say it always. But she must listen, must separately witness my plea for pardon, gift of pardon, our constant death. We both are victim, judge, killer, witness, our simple selves.' "

She has witnessed at least the end of his dream— or heard it, waked at its sound. For the word was actual, spoken aloud. But asleep, she heard the sound not the word; and awake to receive it, she strains to retrieve whatever he has offered, demanded. There is only quiet, the sough of their opposite breaths; but she sees at the window (through blinds, curtains) the signs of day, the world taking hold, the pieces of this room taking their morning places after chaos—chest, chair, table, bed, he flat beside her sounding asleep. She lifts to her right elbow to see; but his black eyes are open, steady, upward. He does not try to meet or avoid her. She thinks he has waked and struggles for his dream. She tells him "You spoke." He nods once slowly. "What did you say? What did you dream?" No nod, waver, flicker of notice. Only his eyelids clamp on themselves as if force would thrust him again into rest. She says, "Go to sleep. We have two hours yet." She falls to her back, turns on her belly, lays on his bare chest her bare left arm. The scars in the hinge of her arm feed there.

FOUR

THE ALCHEMIST

Walking Lessons

WALKING LESSONS

MY WIFE killed herself two weeks ago, her twenty-sixth birthday; and I, not anticipating Christmas at home, wrote to Blix Cunningham (a college friend in VISTA—Volunteers-in-Service-to-America—a med-school dropout, four months short of his degree; he calls it a *pause*) and volunteered to visit him at his post on the Navajo reservation. His reply seemed less eager than his letters eight months before—when he'd landed cold among hostile Indians and urged my wife and me to join him any time—but by then I was grasping any hand extended; so I flew to Albuquerque and rented a car and drove on to him. Dunder, Arizona; half an hour past Gallup off route 66.

Nothing, nothing—a truckstop, a trading post, shoebox post office, the abandoned 1930s tourist cabins in which Blix lives. VISTA volunteers try not to live better than their chosen unfortunates. Blix lives considerably worse than most Navajo (thereby approaching some ultimate in discomfort). Night before last in Albuquerque I stayed in the best motel I've ever seen —everything provided (for $16) but a happy life—and watched TV, the Ed Sullivan Christmas show; a mouse talked Italian and Leontyne Price sang *Vissi d'arte*.

Then last night in Dunder in Blix's two rooms that make Beethoven's study look anal compulsive (old meals petrifying under symphonies, cold pots of piss on the pianolid). He sleeps in the inner room on an iron bed, no sheets but at least an electric blanket. I sleep in the outer room in Blix's sour sleeping bag laid on the springs of an army cot. The only hope of heat against the snow (14° last night) is a potbellied stove in which Blix burns old furniture—and from Dora.

Dora. Dora was there when I arrived. I walked through snow toward the only lighted windows in the ring of ruining cabins, knocked, a wait, then Blix opened on me, as unsurprised as ever—"You made it."

Inside was barely warmer than out and almost as dark. To show I was myself, I made an obscene remark or two on the temperature and decor, my eyes slowly opening to the debris of clothes, sausage cans, books, records (Leontyne Price again, *Porgy and Bess*), wood scraps for the stove, muddy boots, a cherry pie (uncut on the table)—and Dora unmentioned in a corner on a broken chair.

I smiled but didn't speak, suspecting maybe (from her obvious Indianhood) that she wouldn't know English (many Navajo don't). She was nineteen or twenty, lovely not beautiful, standard Indian equipment (enameled black hair and eyes, clearer skin than most, unpocked, a fierce beige).

Then she giggled in response (toward Blix not me) and showed bad teeth, nursed on Coke from the cradle, rotted in a dark perfect crescent in front.

I looked to Blix too and he said "That's Dora" and pointed quickly as though I'd smiled at something else —the cherry pie.

I was hungry, had driven for hours without stopping; so I said, "Dora, did you make the pie?"

She giggled some more till I felt I had landed in a
geisha house—where was her red offended dignity?

Blix said, "No, my landlady did. It's for you. I told
her."

Told her *what*, I didn't ask (nor who landladied
this disaster-site), but to cut the ice, strode forward to
the pie, cut a slice and ate it ravenously—for comic
effect but also to cover my sudden suspicion (dread
colder than the room) that Dora was here for the
night, would stay, and that I must listen.

Two slices of pie were no charm. She stayed. An
hour of tired talk between Blix and me—about nothing: jobs, my trip—then he stood and said, "Bed-
time. You're sleeping on the cot. The bathroom's
there."

Dora headed for the inner room and shut the
cracked door.

Blix went on behind her but stopped once more
and smiled for the first time, "Don't mention this
in Washington"; then lower, in pig-French—"*Je
t'expliquera matin. Elle est en trouble.*"

I worked at guessing what trouble she was in—
through my trip to the bathroom (a cold-water tap and
a john that didn't flush; I leaked out a broken window
into the snow) and back in the dark and seizing cold,
into my sleeping bag. The obvious reading was, she's
pregnant. Who by? Our Volunteer-in-Service-to-Amer-
ica, who else? She'd worn no wedding ring but did any
Navajo? What would Washington do?—send Blix
home to Carolina, no doubt, with Sacajawea and her
copper papoose.

The only sound—above the stove's dying—seemed

confirmation. Not only was she pregnant, they were struggling to abort her. And they worked at it nearly an hour, no pause. I never moved an inch toward their closed cracked door; but I heard every flicker, could hear every impulse leap every synapse—from Blix's slow start, her dark dumb acceptance (they were straining at first for silence—why? sparing me *what?*), onward till they gained a fierce plateau which they held. *Held.* Every nail and joint in the two collapsing rooms was involved, dragooned into their effort.

And I. I did move. When it seemed Blix's gouging would never slacken, no end be reached—release *or* destruction—and that Dora's acceptance swelled more monstrous each moment, I sat upright in my sleeping bag and thought of two things. I could shout to them "Stop!" or, under the cover of their thrusting, I could leave—do my little packing, walk back to my car and, in less than a day, be back in my own house (more ruined than this one would ever be).

So I stayed—stayed in bed, upright, freezing in my underwear but listening. Feeding. Forcing my eyes through the dark, noise and cold; inserting my vision through their door and *among* them. Dipping and probing, diving and stroking and licking between them, around them, above them in their work—till I came to rest in Blix's clenched head and rode out there (battered but helpless to leave, not to share) the rest of the time till they'd reached their yipping yelping end.

—With nothing destroyed, aborted, stove-in. Not even me. I could in fact have killed them—rushed on them *in extremis* with my cherry-pie knife and ended them there (that after all being what they had struggled to offer one another—total vulnerability). One another, though, not me. So I stayed in place, *my* place which they'd assigned me; and silence was all that rushed in on their stillness. No wind outside, the stove cold and mute. I alone awake, upright and listening, my face and the front of my T-shirt wet with tears. (I come from a long line of weepers—never mind. I am going to survive.) Mouth open, still hungry, I fell back and slept.

And didn't wake or turn till, in faint morning light, I heard steps pass me and looked to the outside door to see Dora leaving. No sign of Blix behind her, no noise of a car. So I slept another hour, then woke for good, rose to pee and check on Blix. He was dead-asleep still beneath his hot blanket, coiled against the indoor temperature which must have been well under 20°. I called his name.

He moaned, coiled tighter.

So I went to dress and start a fire, knowing that nothing but a steady din had ever waked Blix. An unexpected transistor radio helped. I flipped it on top-volume and out came a song called "Navajo Sugar-time"—minutes and minutes of heavy tuneless droning by an ancient man in (I take it) Navajo, then a sudden switch to (still tuneless) English for his stunning refrain—

> *Sugar in the morning,*
> *Sugar in the evening,*
> *Sugar at suppertime.*

That routed Blix. He leapt from bed in a single loud stride, flew by me buck-naked with a shameless erection and shouted from the toilet, "They can't even *sing*."

Twenty minutes later we were warm in the truck-stop a mile up the road, eating eggs and sausage beneath a machinemade tapestry of John F. Kennedy; and Blix was volunteering his news, half-whispering—the waitress and cook were Indians. "You're wondering about all that, I guess"—he waved with his hand as though the night were still near, parked just outside. "She's Dora Badonie. Twenty-two. Two kids under five. Their father—her husband, I guess; God knows—is now living with her mother. Maybe *married* to her mother. Sophocles himself would die of surfeit out here —everybody's everybody else's grandmother and is humping her daily. Now she lives with her father in a shack up a wash. But they're better off than most—father works at the trading-post and they have a pickup truck. She does nothing, I guess, but hang around me. I don't *know* that. I don't see all that much of her—that many hours a day. All these people live mysteries, weirder than snakes—what they're thinking or feeling, what they're doing even when they're out of your sight. But I've helped her a little. She was the first one that asked. You remember what I told you it was like at first? I got here ready to pay all debts—mine, the white man's, America's. They wouldn't look at me! Much less speak. It was six or eight weeks of wandering round daily before even the children would wave at me. So there I was in my lush tourist court, alone as a dry bone —and speaking of which, that was fairly desperate too; no help at all, long hours of self-service, pounding time to my five favorite records and "Navajo Sugar Time." Then Dora arrived on the doorstep one morning. I'd

seen her at the trading post. She'd even smiled once—
on those gorgeous teeth—but her father had seen it and
called her down, or said *something* in Navajo. She
never looked again. But here she was, that morning, at
my door. Was I going to Gallup in the next day or so?
"Why?" I said. She said, "There's a baby that's cut his
foot." I knew her father owned a truck and she'd
waked me up; but of course I was weak-kneed with
gratitude—I'd have driven her to Tulsa. So we hauled
her youngest child to Indian hospital—nineteen
stitches; he had dropped his Coke bottle—and after
that she began turning up most every day. Just to sit, at
first—she can barely do more in English than giggle—
then to mend a sock or two. Then to start mending all
my less tangible needs—at my invitation. I still don't
know if it'd crossed her mind before I asked her. I still
don't know if those first two babies weren't virgin
births."

"But this one isn't?" I said.

Blix said "What does that mean?"

"You said she was in trouble when we turned in
last night, and then you proceeded to do about an hour
of demolition on her. I was stunned to see her able to
walk this morning."

Blix pulled at his coffee. "She won't much longer."

"Won't what?"

"Walk."

"Meaning what?" I said.

"Her trouble is multiple sclerosis."

"Since when?" I said.

"Since yesterday. The doctor told her then—
they'd been testing for weeks. She had stopped in to
tell me just before you came."

"No wonder you met me like a sack of dead babies."

"Sorry," Blix said. "I'd hoped to cheer you up."

"It's incurable?"

"She knows that."

"What will she do now?"

"Stay here and die."

"How long will that take?"

"Years. Who knows?"

"What will you do?" I said.

"I don't know," he said. "Are you ready for the next thrill? I had to have a physical myself last week—I'm suspected of having a touch of TB." He gave a little Garbo cough, laughed a little.

But I reached out and stopped him, pressing his wrist. I begged him, "Stay with her." Tears instantly poured. "Don't leave her now."

Blix jerked his wrist free, stared wide-eyed at me as though I were lethal, had powers, could force him. Then he said—aloud at last: the waitress looked up—"Oh Jesus, *I'm* all but cured already!" Then he burst into laughter that seemed so nearly the last thing we shared, so necessary, that I joined him helpless.

The rest of this morning and the early afternoon, we did good deeds. Or tried to do them. Or tried to discover what deeds needed doing, then wheedle the numerous permissions to do them. Someone had told Blix the day before that an Indian named Atso had been sick in bed for over a week and needed food and firewood. Blix had waited till this morning, he said (I asked), for several reasons—he'd been told after dark and didn't want to risk getting snowbound with his truck (four-wheel drive though it is) three miles off the highway up a steep arroyo; this Atso was a drunk, that was his trouble (a weeklong drunk) and Blix was sick of running taxi service for hopeless winos. His aims had been higher. This morning the problem was sun—a thaw. The washes would be mud.

But we made it very slowly, up a ditch deep in mud between pink cliffs, all bare as the moon and so beautiful, profuse, as to be unnoticeable—an occasional plant neither of us could name, odd strips of barbed wire surrounding nothing and the standard-issue dead coyote (defrosting, collapsing inward on himself but grinning to the last). Then the Atsos—my first hogan. Round, of mud and logs, a domed roof cut by a stove pipe dissolving in rust, it seemed a low but immortal growth implored from the ground by protracted bellowings (hunching gyrations, gashings, blood) from the wretched of the earth—the only gift they would ever receive, except cur dogs (three groveled at the door) and their adamant faces. And government food—the yard was strewn with cans of white man's food they would only feed to dogs: string beans, dried milk. And our little grudging visit, mine and Blix's.

Blix went in, through the barking dogs, past the dwarf oblivious grandmother spreading quilts on a line (quilts *made* of dirt).

I waited in the truck. Blix had said it would be hard enough doing business without me along, a fresh white stranger. So to pass the time, I filled out a form for a Carte Blanche credit card (I mean—I'll *need*—to make a lot more trips). Then—no sign of Blix, just me and the dogs, the mud and the quilts, pinyon and snow

and sandstone cliffs—I defaced the application by writing lines on the clean backside:

> *Ten yards to my left an Indian man—*
> *age 30, alcoholic, Navajo—*
> *lies locked in unknown illness, silence, calm.*
>
> *My friend—whose job it is—yearns patiently*
> *to comprehend, heal ancient various wounds;*
> *gives solemn smiles, shows new-grown neck-length*
>   *curls.*
>
> *I stay outside beside the truck's strong heater,*
> *complete my application for* Carte Blanche—
> Income? *I write in* Thirty thousand dollars,
> *growl at the Indian's dog, begin this poem.*

I'm cheating, you'll say—"You were thinking
then, alone there and idle." What was I thinking? Do I
have human feelings?—his wife freshly dead and he
two thousand miles from home at Christmas on an
Indian reservation the size of West Virginia (and twice
as miserable), his only two companions struck with
maybe fatal diseases? If you've followed me this far,
you'll be grumbling for such answers. And a good many
more—*why did she do it?* Wait; please, wait. Remember, Tolstoy tells you only two or three facts about the
life of Anna before the book's *present.* I'm struggling
to tread the waters of the present. Tread with me or
sink (or swim back out—simply shut the book). The
present is my story. The rest is waiting.

In fact, at the time, I wasn't thinking. The manual
labor (application, poem) took care of conscious
thought—analysis, self-pity. In its own way, each ges-

ture now is desperate, each step a kind of busy-work. The unconscious was whirring away, no doubt—because, by the end of the poem, I was *feeling*. The inside of my skin was rapidly furring (a sick child's tongue) with unfocused misery; and I was considering disobeying orders—entering the hogan. At least I'd have sights, new grist for the eyes.

But Blix appeared, fast and furious. He tore the door open, climbed in, gripped the steering wheel and shook it as though he were tetanizing. No glance at me, no word.

"All dead?" I asked.

Another siege of spasms, a long wait—"Yes, goddammit."

I was ready to think he had cut their throats. "Be serious."

He laughed. "No, but everybody's sick as dogs—*except* the dogs and that old woman. Atso's not drunk—sober as you—but he and three kids are baking with fever and nobody can—or will—speak two words of English. They don't trust me so there's no chance of hauling them all to Gallup. They want a medicine ceremony—they haven't got ten cents to buy dry beans —and I, being me, don't even own an aspirin. Dr. Cunningham." By then he had calmed. He was galvanized, on-stage, a clear duty at hand. He sat awhile longer, then said, "I'm sorry. We've got to do this—I'll go to Window Rock to get a tribal nurse. If I try to phone her, she'll never find the place. With the roads this muddy, that'll take four hours. But will you wait here?—at my place, I mean? I'm supposed to be visited sometime today by the thinly-disguised regional spy from VISTA. You can tell him I'm at work, saving

lives Hell for leather—you'll even have a share in this
glorious work. Then, as reward, when I get back and
we've stocked the Atsos' pantry, we can go in to Gallup
for a gourmet meal—cold grease tacos—and an Ann-
Margret movie."

"Click heels," I said and smiled; but as we drove
off, I rushed into dread. Had I run all this way to turn
now and make my stand among cold debris (half a
cherry pie) in a 6′ x 8′ abandoned tourist court in the
Arizona desert?

I had. Yes.

Blix barely stopped but handed me the key and,
over the loud engine, said, "There's lots of books and
records. If you'll clean house, you'll find them."

I cleaned as though they were the walls of my
head—the two wrecked rooms—as though every misplaced letter, sock, can, were a clot of contagion that
could kill if not forced into place at once. (*Kill* by a
kind of sympathetic magic—by forcing my head to
acknowledge its own mess. Seductive and true but
avoidable.) Well, I fired the stove and then I forced it
into place—the two rooms' freight of junk, every disordered atom. Half the battle was finding the places—
Blix had no sense of any object's place—so I ruthlessly
defined all his space as to *function*. All clothing, shoes,
birthcontrol apparel in the inner room (where I made
Blix's bed—no sheets; he had none—by smoothing the
blanket on the mattress stiff with waste). All scrap
wood and paper in the corner by the stove. All un-
opened cans, cereal boxes, two mugs in an opposite corner. All records, books, letters and magazines by the two

usable chairs in the center of the room where I had slept. Then I scoured the wash basin, poured Clorox in the john. Then I swept all the floors (several pints of mouse turds). Then I thought of scrubbing. No wet mop or brush or bucket for water. (All the place had been scrubbed of was medical equipment—not an aspirin, as he'd said; no trace of his mammoth delicate training, his former purpose pursued with a force that drills bedrock, in which he'd paused.)

But by then—an hour—I was calmer, safer. When the VISTA spy came, he'd find sanity, space. I could take a little walk, still in sight of the road; but the sun shone on, only deepening the mud and I had no boots, only suede ankleshoes. I'd buy real boots tonight in Gallup. I was safe enough to sit now, hear music, rest and read. Leontyne Price again, lobbing great silver spinning frisbees into air, each note above A more curative than the last, but vanishing. And Kluckhohn and Leighton's book *The Navaho*. I skimmed the tragic history (all the Trails of Tears) and economics and settled more slowly into Chapter 5, "The Supernatural: Power and Danger." By the time I reached the subheading "Ghosts," I was reading—consuming—every word:

> *The Navahos seem to have no belief in a glorious immortality. Existence in the hereafter appears to be only a shadowy and uninviting thing. The afterworld is a place like this earth, located to the north and below the earth's surface. It is approached by a trail down a hill or cliff, and there is a sandpile at the bottom. Deceased kinfolk, who look as they did when last seen alive, come to guide*

the dying to the afterworld during a journey
that takes four days. At the entrance to the
afterworld, old guardians apply tests to see if
death has really occurred.

Death and everything connected with it
are horrible to The People . . .

Most of the dead may return as ghosts to
plague the living. Only those who die of old
age, the stillborn, and infants who do not live
long enough to utter a cry or sound do not
produce ghosts, and for them the four days of
mourning after burial need not be observed,
since they will not be injurious to the living.
Otherwise, any dead person, no matter how
friendly or affectionate his attitude while he
was living, is a potential danger.

A ghost is the malignant part of a dead
person. It returns to avenge some neglect or
offense . . .

I broke off there, turned to the index—*Suicide.*
Two references—the first unnourishing: a man had
shot the witches who killed his children, then had
killed himself. The second though was this:

Indeed, except for the (by no means
universally accepted) view that witches and
suicides live apart in the afterworld, there is
no belief that the way one lives on earth has
anything to do with his fate after death.

I am twenty-eight years old, a well-trained teacher
of college English, a would-be poet and novelist who
has not been to church (Episcopal) since age nineteen;
but I said then—aloud, I'm sure aloud—"They do,

they *should*." And I felt the need to know how *far* apart, in what kind of place, and how are they punished? Maybe the wretched Navajo have learned what *I* know, what all of Virgil, Aquinas and Florence couldn't teach Dante who discovers suicides in the Seventh Circle only (as brown, stooped and fruitless trees that exhude poison, or blood if torn). The Ninth, the *Ninth* Circle! Sealed, up-ended in perpetual ice—as "Traitors to Their Kin," even gnashed forever in the triple mouths of Satan as "Traitors to Their Lords and Benefactors." Judas, Brutus, Cassius had the kindness at least to *kill* their lords, not leave them behind alive, abandoned, dumb with guilt and mystery, unable to answer the final indictment flung at the living by a suicide.

But I read every word on witches and ghosts and found nothing else to my need or purpose. Blix would not be back for maybe two hours. I fed the stove again, came back to the stack of tattered books I'd arranged, glanced through them again, then took up the only thing I wanted—the pack of letters which, oddly, Blix had kept together, neatly rubberbanded. His news from outside, proofs of another life, answers. I sorted them furtively. The top half-dozen were clearly Christmas cards, two letters from his mother, mine announcing the death and my arrival. I had not read a word yet, beyond the postmarks—not even my own (there were six or eight; I'm a good correspondent). If I'd read my most recent you'd have known the bare facts by now— so soon!—but I didn't, not because I was already shaping my day as a Work of Art—a Joan Crawford movie: Joan reads us a letter, voice-over, leaves blowing—but because I was sparing myself all I could. *Sparing!*—

two-thirds through the stack, my wife's hand. The standard rotund upright hand of the 1940s American girl—but hers without a doubt, her heavyweight blue paper, our postmark, November.

I set the other letters down (I'd yet to read one) and studied hers (the envelope, the *object*). Blix had opened it neatly, top-edge, with a knife; most others he'd torn open any crude way. And it had not been crushed, as most others had, by a full day's work in his Levi hip-pocket. It was fresh and clearly valued, like an invitation, a girl's souvenir. Personal property. I was calmer then than I'd been in days, maybe since the day. I'm sure I felt no trace of suspicion—that the letter contained secret news; she and Blix had hardly met. Nor of pity for her, myself—nor Blix, Dora, the sick Mr. Atso and his hungry children. Only anger, disgust —all as cold and contained as this room could make them; maybe 40°—and curiosity. How could they do it? Any one of them, not to mention the twos?

The music had stopped and I set her letter down, on top of the others, and began to stand. More music. Price again—"Summertime" (Hear it, if you haven't, in an unheated shack in late December; you'll have *heard* it at last). But I knew I could neither return and read her letter nor replace it unread in Blix's little pack, not at the edge of the music. I sat back and read it.

> *Dear Blix,*
> *This is meant to bring light to your life. Your letter seemed so lost that I've thought of you all morning as our man on the moon, or in some satellite gone out of control and circling, perfect but irretrievable.*

You can come back if you want to,
though. Life's a plane-ride away. Familiar life.
If you want it, come back. But you left be-
cause you didn't. You're old enough to know.
So am I. Don't think of it as quitting. Do
what you need to do and if no one under-
stands, so what? forever. I'll understand—and
still so what?—

That was her last whole sentence. I saw it had a
close, a perfunctory "Love" and her name. I couldn't
look at those, can't yet take her name but must treat it
for now (for my own clear reasons) as my personal
Tetragrammaton—the name of unspecified punishment, permanent damage; not love. I listened to the
room, the road outside—not a sound; I'd raided Blix's
mail in secret.

For what? Not a gram of revelation. A girl at the
lip of suicide writes a letter that might have come from
—Eleanor Roosevelt, sensible, bland, a little senten-
tious. And yet, to my knowledge, the last page of
writing she ever did, beyond grocery memos, checks.
But no note—to me or the lethal world at large. What
would I have wanted? If she'd asked me to draft a final
message, from her to me, what would I have said?—*I'm*
as sorry as you need me to be. All debts canceled. So
what? she said to Blix. Can I say it to her? So what?—
nothing adds up to a suicide, nothing leads down from
it. Apart in the afterworld—Amen.

Someone knocked at the door. The VISTA spy.
Good. Another *event;* he'd be good for half an hour.
But I opened on Dora, ten yards away, already leaving.

At my sound, she stopped and turned and faced

me broadside—a girl five-foot-two in a boy's thin poplin windbreaker, tan skirt, white sneakers, white socks, grave as the gymnasts her get-up resembled. And as tense and reluctant.

And powerful—I could not simply say Blix was gone and let her leave (she was on foot, in snow and mud, no sign of her truck). I called her by name and said "Come in."

She stood on awhile, serious as before, her sneakers blotting up dirty water. She was studying me.

"Remember me?" I said.

She nodded—no more giggling—as though she remembered more than she'd seen. My role in last night's loving.

"Then come in. It's dry at least."

She came and walked past me through the room now miraculously clean since morning and took a place, standing, at the far wall near the window. If she'd noticed the cleaning, she gave no sign.

I asked her to sit in the chair I'd just warmed, but she shook her head No. I thought we might be up against a taboo on women sitting while men still stood, so I sat in the broken chair and again said "Sit down." She refused again but this time she giggled and I felt we could talk. She had shown no curiosity whatever about Blix's whereabouts, had not glanced to right or left—maybe she could *smell* his absence—so I started with that. "Blix has gone to Window Rock to get a nurse for a man that's sick—Atso."

She said "I know that."

"Did you see him on the way?"—in which case, I wondered, why are you here with me?

"No. Atso's been sick."

"What's his trouble?" I said.

"Tokay wine," she said, serious again. Then she said—she was facing me—"I got trouble too."

I was trapped (by the word) into thinking she meant herself, her multiple sclerosis; and in a quick hail of amazement (that she, the Silent American, was telling it to me—after all though, we'd spent a fairly close night together)—and gratitude and because my own heart was so compressed inside me, I said "So do I."

She took a step forward—necessarily toward me —and said "You hungry?"

Every exit from my body was instantly clogged, not with tears this time but with more gratitude—a great rush of gratitude, like birds from a cave, toward this small girl who, dying, thought trouble was hunger. I stood and took a quick step toward her.

She held ground, neither inviting me onward nor repelling me. She seemed to have decided from the moment she entered that she was mine to use, whoever I was, whatever I might choose. Her face had the patience of landscape—rocks, trees. *This* landscape, of course.

Pausing, I knew she was right. It was well past noon. I was very hungry. Hunger was sculpting my face from inside; I felt dangerously lean. So I said "Yes, hungry."

"You like Vienna sausage?"

"Yes."

"He always eat sausage."

I thought she would move to fix me a meal but she stayed in place. She had made the diagnosis, suggested the cure. Now over to me. I found a small can of

sausages—food-corner—opened them and extended the
can to her, across the whole room.

She smiled, shook her head and went back to the
window, to watch the road.

I sat and ate the sausages, then stood to get the
cherry pie. She stood so still and expectantly—but for
Blix, I thought—that I'd watched her whole minutes
before recognizing a "situation," this hour's dilemma.
Blix had said not to mention her "in Washington";
should I tell her now that the spy was expected and let
her flee (leaving me alone again) to return at all-clear
(tonight, for another jamboree) or should I let her
stand on there to greet the spy and earn Blix his
reprimand, maybe his walking papers? The abandonment of her.

I sat, with the pie, and said to myself, "If she gives
some sign before I finish the pie, I'll help her—or warn
her, whether that's help or not." I had no idea what a
sign would be, and I'd got almost to the deadline—silence.

Then—not turning, still her back, still waiting for
something—she said, "That's all you meant?—you
hungry?"

I had meant a good deal more—ten minutes before, in mentioning trouble; but her very presence with
me had dispersed that jam. My needs now were toward
her. But the only help seemed *warning*, not a heart-to-
heart cry. I said, "Dora, Blix asked me to wait here
while he's gone. He's expecting a visit from a vista
man. Any minute now."

She waited, not turning, but all her force seemed
flowing toward the door, to leave, take cover. "I know
that," she said—her *I* the first word she'd accented

since I'd known her.

"Blix told you?" I asked.

She nodded Yes but kept her place.

So tables were turned. I was no longer driving, if I ever had—no longer sparing lovers. That she knew and was staying, was the new dilemma. Right. I'd also stay and watch—an independent citizen, let Washington beware.

And I'd no more than eaten the last of the pie when Dora turned to face me and said "He's coming."

"Blix?"

"The other man."

There seemed a quick note of alarm in her voice and, rising, I thought, "What other man?—her father? husband? lover?" Was I lured to the brink of my debut (or Act II?) in melodrama?—shot or stabbed as a rival for the love of a girl with bad teeth and multiple sclerosis? So what? Who would mind? A knock at the door. I looked back to Dora—inscrutable—then advanced, really half expecting Fate.

A white man in an army surplus jacket, thirty-two maybe, already balding. He was straining—in the face of a stranger: me—not to smile; but with his face, as full, fed and deeply incurious as a baby's bottom, formality was hopeless. I knew at once he'd go no farther than hurt feelings, bafflement.

He said, "My name's Tim Neely. Is Blixford Cunningham still registered here?" He surrendered then, tried to smile but laughed.

So I laughed along and said, "He's gone to Window Rock—an emergency—to get a tribal nurse for a sick man here. He asked me to stay here and meet you if you came."

"Good," he said. "Good."

I asked him in, not knowing whether Dora would have fled through a window or be hiding under the bed.

She was where I had left her—where she'd been last night, when I arrived; her receiving-post.

And like me last night, Neely didn't seem to see her though the lines of vision were uncluttered now. Before I could try to introduce her, he saw the finished pie plate—"Blix has gone in for baking, eh?"

I said, "Yeah, that's been our Christmas"; then I offered him instant coffee.

He accepted and while I was warming the hot-plate, I saw him see her. I could make a lot of cheap jokes at his expense—I've tried a few already, the itiner-ant do-gooder working through Christmas, breathless with *hope*—but now I was with him. Suddenly he was "on," all his resources summoned, every course he'd ever taken. I could see tact and patience, sweet defer-ence, bubbling up in him like spring water through sand—had he met her before? did he know the whole story or any part? Was that why he was here today—boom-lowering?

There was no way to guess from Dora's face—she was doing her piece-of-nature stunt again. Or was her face already slightly sclerotic?

Neely turned back to me—the kettle knocked with heat—"It's sure been a cleanup campaign in here. Who do we have to thank?"

I took that as a straw flung kindly to the drowning. I nodded toward Dora—"Her. Thank her. That's Dora Badonie."

He exhaled visible relief—I was playing-up grand; why were fellows like me not Volunteers? He could now speak to Dora—"Well, thank you a lot. You been helping Blix out?"

No giggle. "I live here."

The rooms seemed instantly vacuumed, utterly empty. We all seemed about to be sucked against the walls at ferocious comic speeds.

Neely broke the lock—a little puff through his nose, his try at a chuckle. "Which Badonie are you? Who's your father round here?"

She was merciless. "No. Here." Then she smiled not giggled.

I wanted to harm her, lunge against her, strike her —above all, to *stop* her. Whatever she was launched on was harmful itself—at the worst, shipping Blix out of here in disgrace (worse still, her with him, paralyzing daily); at the least, embarrassing this well-intentioned man. It was in my mouth to say "She's lying."

But Neely spoke first, to Dora not me—"I know. I know a lot." Then he turned to me. "What are you in all this?"

His sudden attempt to switch the controls—from Friendly Equal to Steely Superior—drew it from me. "I'm a poor unfortunate cripple seeking help."

I'd kept a straight face so he had to pursue; I was in his field now. He looked me over for a gimp-leg or arm, then said "What help?"

"Are you married?" I said.

"Yes."

"Your wife nearby?"

"Back in Gallup with the kids." He actually pointed east.

"Then tell me please—you're older than me— what kind of help would you plan to need if you got home tonight—what time will that be?"

"Soon as I see Blix."

"—Well, five o'clock, say; it'll still be light. What
help will you need at five o'clock today when you get
home and find little what's-her-name stretched dead on
the floor, drained dry as a kosher chicken?"

Neely licked his lips; I was baking him out! Then,
helpless, he smiled—reflexes dying hard. "Hold on a
minute, friend. There are laws against you; threats are
frowned on by the law"—still smiling, a struggle to josh
his way clear. "Anyhow, we're not Jewish."

"Sorry," I said. "You asked who I was."

He said, "OK, you told me." Then he walked
toward the door, had his hand on the latch before
stopping again. "I'm not waiting here. Tell Blix Cunningham to phone me collect, by noon tomorrow."

"Does he know your number?"

He had shed all his roles, was down to a core,
could stand on its firmness. "He knows everything he
needs to know. Even knows what's coming." He
opened the door.

"Wait," I said. "Mr. Neely, I'm sorry if I've acted
rudely. I *am* in trouble—"

He waited long enough for me to feel the second
law of thermodynamics stage a demonstration round us
—my scarce, nurtured heat rushing headlong through
the door. Then he said, "You're one of millions, son"
and obeyed the law himself.

His car had cranked and gone before I turned to
Dora. She was pressed against the window to watch
him go; but when my staring turned her, I said "What
was that for?"

"What?"

"Your lie."

"No lie," she said. She walked to the open door of Blix's bedroom. "I sleep here every night before you came." Her voice had hardly altered—soft, uninflected —but a new hard vehemence thrust up in her stance, the words themselves. She paused for air and when I had not answered—assent or challenge—she half-turned and pointed to the bed behind her. "Come here. I'll show you."

I was locked down suddenly in the sense of enacting my old ended life, of facing a ghost—*"the malignant part of a dead person."*

So—whoever she was—she said again *"Here."*

I'm a human at least, not a Skinnerized dog. I said, "No, I made that bed; I've seen all you can show."

"Please come," she said—a change of words not tone.

I said, "I'll give evidence—eyewitness evidence—in any court you name that you've spent any number of hours right there, stretched flat of your back, hauling Blix's ashes."

She didn't understand; I was glad of that much. In a moment she could smile. "You're funny." Then a wait—"You're in trouble too, you tell him?"—she pointed after Neely.

"My wife—you know."

"You married?" she said.

"Well, no more," I said. I thought she was probing—not for news but to punish me.

"Where's your wife now?"

"In the Navajo afterworld—off to one side."

"I don't understand."

I saw that she didn't. "Blix hasn't told you?"

"He don't tell me nothing."

I said "My wife is dead," half hoping to leave it there.

"Oh," she said; her hands did one silent flap at her sides, as though they were vestigial wings that had tried once more to fly. Then—"Having a baby?"

I knew I was glad. I would get to tell her—some human at least (Blix had yet to mention it). That would be for me—pressure released—but what could and would it be for Dora?—terror? compulsion to shelter me, love me? or a crushing memento of her own creeping death? I said, "No. No babies; we never had babies. She didn't want babies. No, she killed herself."

It pulled her one step forward toward me—three steps between us now—and her small dark head made a twisting thrust, as though to bring nearer still her eyes, ears (lips? do they kiss? it's not in the book). Her face gave no signal of feeling or intention—I was nodding, helpless—then something deflected her. Something from me, or her, or elsewhere. She turned, as though I were The Road Not Taken, and went back to her window and looked out awhile.

Nothing passed, we were freezing, I must feed the stove.

Then she faced me again and asked—really *asked*, with misplaced inflection, but pressed by need— "*When* she killed herself?"

I'd planned to say *how*, but I gave what she wanted. "Two weeks ago. It's why I'm here with Blix" —here with frigid empty air!—"I thought he would've told you."

She was off Blix for now. "She was real old, your wife?"

"Twenty-six."

"Oh," she said. "She was real sick?"

"Yes."

"What kind?"

"Well, her head."

"What you mean?" Again she was pressed.

I couldn't think what phrase she'd know or, then, what would say at least part of what I meant without baffling or blinding her. So I said "Mentally ill."

"She don't know what she was doing to herself?"

Was that part, at all, of what I'd meant?—or felt or believed? I said, "Maybe not. Maybe she thought it wouldn't work—not completely, not death; just enough to hurt and warn me. A pistol in the mouth."

Dora didn't understand, not even the words. Her face had made again that half-screw forward.

But I wouldn't stop now; this was not for Dora now—"She knew this much—what she was doing to *me.*"

Dora said "I got to go," but she stayed in place.

"Don't," I said. "Please."

She nodded fiercely. "Yeah. I got to go."

I said "Come here. Please."

She said "I got to get Blix."

"He's gone—why?"

"He'll help me. I got trouble."

"*I* know that," I said. "He told me this morning."

"He don't know this morning. I don't know it then."

I'd given up understanding—interlingual misfires. I said "Well, wait. Come here."

She looked to see where I meant—I'd pointed nowhere. The army cot? sleeping bag? the clean-swept floor?

I didn't know either but I saw her, after what

seemed a soundless subaqueous hour, begin oaring to me through the room's thick air.

Blix of course arrived then—the truck in the yard (by its clashing gears), the actual sound of his boots in the slush (through walls, our bones), his height and face in the doorway beside us.

Dora hadn't heard him. She was aimed on me—three more steps to take.

But Blix never noticed, locked as he was in the newest defeat—neither Dora nor the clean room nor however she and I stood, drawing one another. Face white, he said (to the room more than us), "Are you ready for this?—I drive to Window Rock and the nurse is at Chinle. She may can come tomorrow, if the roads dry a little—to bathe the corpse! Now I'll have to go to Atso's again—take food to those children, tell him to wait. But he's good at that." He was turning to leave again—follow if we wished. Had he yet seen Dora? Was she visibly there?

She said "Help *me*."

Blix stopped, looked a moment. "Help you do what?"

"I got trouble," she said.

"I know that," he said. "I told you No."

"This is new," she said and she looked to me.

I'd really never meant to cause Blix further worry, never needed or intended to slosh my own woe; so I braced for Dora's latest inscrutable lurch—denunciation? cry-rape? whatever.

She said, "My truck. My grandma took it up the Zuni road last night and my brother come down to tell me this morning—she got it stuck up there."

That's the trouble?" Blix said. "That's all I've got

to do?—feed a starving dying family, then drive fifty miles in foot-deep mud and unstick your truck? Two more days of sun, a little wind—you'll be able to drive it out on your own." He took another step, to go to Atso.

I moved to follow, having soloed and dueted enough for one day.

But before we could reach the door and pause for Dora, she said loudly "No."

We both looked—tears. They were pouring through our silence. I wanted to rush past Blix—bail-out.

But he blocked the way. He studied her a moment, then said gravely "No what?"

She said "Help me."

He broke, for the second time today, into total laughter; and relieved to see him that free (or desperate), I joined, loudly.

Dora stood on in tears, bathing her troubles.

But he helped her. (*Why?*) Of necessity, *we* helped her—I being determined not to spend another minute alone in those rooms today. We drove to the trading post (no sign of Dora's father), bought groceries for Atso (Blix paid) and we left Dora—to look for more men to help us with her truck. Then we wallowed back to Atso's—the tracks half-again as deep in mud as this morning—and again I waited alone in the truck for the minutes Blix took to leave the food and attempt to explain that a nurse would come tomorrow, wait one more night.

I only had five minutes (Blix was rushing now—

toward what? and for whom?); but I worked at questions, nagged at them, dog-like—neither Dora nor I had mentioned Neely's visit and Blix had not yet asked. Should I wait till he asked or tell him now, in our last few minutes alone today (describing Dora's gambit); or should I just say "Neely says phone him"?

Not till I saw his face emerging from the hogan—firmed with purpose, locked into senseless duties, *happy* against his better wishes to have fed a sick drunk for one more day and assured him of help in a foreign tongue—did I know: say nothing. Wait. His life, not mine; he must ask all the questions, invent his own threats, secrete his own solutions, make his own errors freely. I, in any case, am safe—in this one corner of my stunned life. Blix and Dora are separate; they are not me.

He didn't ask (has he really forgot or does he not want to know?); but to give him the chance, I rode in silence; and when he did speak, it was now, at last, to include me in his purpose, his new grip on life, his charity (I am not ironic; I'm seriously needy). He said my name—which in itself startled me (he'd not said it before, I realized; eight months with the Navajo and he had their fear of using any man's name).

I faced him across the long empty space.

But he faced the road—or the track he was struggling to lay through mire—and said, "Do you want me to ask you any questions?" (He only possessed the barest facts, from my last letter to him.)

I said, "Ask. I'll answer some. Some I won't know. Some I'm not up to tackling."

If he'd had questions ready, that threw him into silence. Or maybe it was only his struggle with the mud.

So I turned from him and tried to watch the famous scenery. Surely solace waited there for the lacerated spirit? Rainbow colors; stones, even plants, the shape of the light; God's imagination pressed by the local conditions (self-imposed in His case) to an effort, say, as total in its perverse triumph over limitations as Michelangelo's on the Sistine's architecture, Beethoven's over the human voice. (*Lesson:* I could do it too. *Question:* Why should I?)

Blix had found his tongue—ithyphallic in tension —"How *alone* do you feel?"

Long as I've known him, I wouldn't have given him credit for that much—to rock me off-balance with the Compassionate Unexpected, verbal pentothal. I found of course that I welcomed the dose and without calculation, said, "Fairly completely. But I don't much mind. That's hardly recent."

Blix nodded. "No company?"

I said, "Aunts and uncles, a few colleagues, neighbors with casseroles"—then realized he was on detective duty: *was adultery at the bottom? catting round again?* So I said, "But no, less company than you've got here, by one precisely."

He smiled—on my side of his face at least—at the puncture of his tactic. Then he struck for the heart. "What was it about?"

My sources on suicide are not entirely limited to the Navajo overview. Masochistic as it's been, the books I left behind on the bedside table were Durkheim's *Suicide* and Menninger's *Man Against Himself*. So I gave the readiest answer—"She wanted to kill somebody, she chose herself, and—the key to her success was—she also wanted to *die*. Hence the pistol —rare for women."

He said "That's what you believe?"

I said "You know it's not."

"Had she warned you ever?"

"From the day I met her. She'd been issuing warnings since she learned to talk, since she learned to move (eyes, hands)—she never spoke them."

"Did she leave a note?" he said.

"Not to me. Not a word."

"To anybody else?"

"If so, they haven't told me."

He said "That's something."

"How?"

"What's not written is easier forgot."

I said "Think again."

He said "OK," which I took for kindness; but after the last few yards of mud, the highway regained, the grind of the four-wheel drive reduced, he said "What comes next?"

"In what?" I said—"this day, this conversation?"

"Your life," he said.

It issued, ruptured. I regretted every syllable that rushed my teeth—"Are you the man to ask that?—Mr. Ambition, Clear-Sight, Dr. Steady-Aim?"

He was quick but calm. "No, but you're here. You've always been aimed before; God knows, on-target far more times than me—"

"Block your metaphor," I said. "The target succumbed. But I know, Blix; I'm sorry. I'm just treading water—no signs in the sea."

"You'll make it," he said. As though it were a fact as dry and indisputable as a grain of rice.

Blix has such impeccable credentials as a man whose lips never touched a lie that I had to say "What makes you sure?"

For the moment, his tone (still loose in the truck), his unsmiling profile seemed to promise a chart, a followable plan which he now possessed and offered to give. But he said, "Because it's all you've wanted."

"What's *it?*" I asked.

"To be scraped, like you are, bare—owing nobody life, help or any piece of you. Did you ever *come* for her, ever donate that much?—a teaspoon as rich as Eagle-Brand milk of all your precious life-codes treading cream? Or is that secret too?—being saved for *who?*"

I said, "Who do you suggest? Name somebody—Dora?"

"Good as any," Blix said. "Take her—my blessing. She'll be ready when we round this curve right here. Look up on the left, any second now! Just say 'Dora, follow me' and she'll follow, forever. No wait—no going home to get the kids or say goodbye, no toothbrush to pack. And a taboo on suicide—of course, she's petrifying."

I said "Stop." I meant the truck—stop and let me out. I would walk to my car and head for home.

But Blix thought I meant his speech and did stop that, as we rounded his curve on Dora, ready.

I dreaded that he might pursue his urging in Dora's presence—be converted, by his own life and the nearness of mine, to monstrosity.

He stopped in the mud by the gas pump however and, as Dora came toward us, said quietly "Just a minute." He got down and said four words to her, then went to the back to pump his own gas.

Dora opened the driver's door and climbed up the high step to sit beside me—so close (already, with Blix not there to crowd us) that I had a quick thought of contagion—she'd infect me—and pressed against my door.

But she said "We got help" and pointed out the window at a knot of people advancing on the truck—four Indian men, all five-foot six, all in khaki pants, not a coat among them (white and blue shirtsleeves) and a single woman (more nearly a girl) in a Pendleton blanket, machinemade, green, dirty and hideous. The men walked in mud as though it were pavement (or familiar at least, if miserable); the girl lurched.

I asked "Who are they?" and turned to look through the small rear window into the tarpaulined truck-bed where they hoisted and jerked and shunted one another.

Dora said "My brothers."

I could see the girl groping at a man's hip pocket for a bottle, and the bottle's label as she seized it, studied it a moment—LAIRD'S STRAIGHT APPLE BRANDY. "Who's the girl?" I asked.

Dora said "Somebody's wife."

I stared on backwards—which poor somebody? The girl had leaned against the rear of the cab and was sucking off a good inch of brandy, raw. She'd have emptied it—and still been unappeased; a face like a gully, that famished and demanding—if the man who seemed to own it hadn't wrenched it down from her. The bottle socked her teeth; I heard it through plate-glass. The other three men laughed; the girl bawled and rocked in misery.

I asked, "What help are they going to be?"

Still not looking, Dora smiled. "They're strong. And they want to go home."

"Where's that?"

"Up where my truck was trying to go—my grandma's; there." She pointed rightward, across the highway toward the line of low hills in middle distance, pink where the sun had begun stripping snow.

"Why are they down here, then?"

"Looking round."

Blix opened his door, climbed in and sat. He cranked, then said—toward the glass but to Dora— "This is our help?"

"Yep." She smiled.

"The girl's pregnant—right?"

"I guess so—yep."

"God bless her," he said and shifted into gear.

"—*Us*," I said. I was looking across Blix and Dora toward the store.

A man had rushed out and was loping toward us —an Indian, tall, his white hair banded by a blue forehead rag in the old style, face all but bursting with barely-held fury. Geronimo.

Blix seemed not to notice and engaged the clutch.

But Dora said "Wait; my daddy" and nodded.

Blix looked, depressed his foot and waited, straining for calm but betraying fear—when the man had stopped a foot from the truck, a foot from Blix's face, his windowglass was still tight shut.

So the man simply waited, staring down.

"Roll the glass," Dora said.

Blix rolled it down, took Badonie's first look and tried the Navajo greeting (one of his three phrases)— "*Yah-ta-hey*."

Badonie said only "You going to Gallup?"

Blix said "Yes—passing through."

Badonie stepped nearer—the last step available before cold steel—but turned his back and looked toward the store—a long wood bench bearing five old Indians, three women, two men. One man wore the old high-crowned black hat and held a pint-bottle, half-full on his knee. Two of the women watched it—its guardians or threats? The third woman—separate—watched the air before her, past us, the south hills. Among pure misery, she condensed a purer brand—no mixture, no compound: Silent Pain. Badonie faced Blix again and pointed toward her. "That old woman yonder has been waiting two days to go in to town. She been sick and her son-in-law—he's a Navajo policeman—said he'd pick her up here and take her to the hospital. So she walked to here yesterday morning early—from way back that way, five or six miles—and he didn't never come. She waited all night and all day today. He hadn't never come."

It was offered as fact, with the veiled passivity of subject peoples. The Negroes of my childhood would come like that, to the backdoor at night, with some tale of woe—someone's shot, cut, dying; then would stop and stand silent. You would think they were waiting, confident in the cunning of their desperation; but at bottom, they were not. They were calmly, utterly, hopeless. They had merely told the truth, had been impelled to come not so much in need or expectation of help as in the simple—simple!—wish to tell a story: *this is what's happening; I want you to know.* Then if you acted—said "Climb in the car" or "I'll get the doctor"—your act was accepted with, again, calm grace, not as due response but as miracle (miracles were not infrequent), a blessing detached.

Badonie seemed now to stand like that—as the old woman sat—beyond hope or pride; and when Blix said "I'll take her," he said "OK" and, not going to her to help or explain, he called out to her in Navajo.

In maybe ten seconds—the time it took to reach her—she stood and started toward us.

Dora said, "Mae Clain. She just got rheumatism."

The woman was moving to the back of the truck; so Blix climbed down and said to Badonie, "Tell her to come up here."

He did and she came and—the two men standing back—she struggled up the step and onto the seat beside Dora, twelve inches from me. She at once faced forward—a face as text-book Indian as the Buffalo Nickel's, seamed as skirts on Egyptian statues, the oiled black hair scraped tightly back (not a white strand in it) yet impossible to date. Sixty-five? Eighty-five? either or neither. Her only sound was shallow breath, labored from her climb; her only admission of kinship with us (even with Dora who touched her) was the high scary odor that leeched from her rapidly as hemorrhaging blood. Made of metal like us but an older grade whose hardness shames.

Dora also didn't speak or look—some clan taboo? —and when Blix remounted, neither did he. (I glanced quickly back—our helpers were oblivious, tussling round their bottle.) He looked out at Dora's father still.

Badonie said, "OK. You going to town?" He had never acknowledged Dora. She lived with him.

"Now," Blix said.

"She got a daughter live in town somewhere"—he seemed to mean Mae Clain not Dora; but he gave no

directions, again made no connection. He held up his
hand to Blix's open window, a little package in it. I
could read the label—SKOAL WINTERGREEN FLAVORED
CHEWING TOBACCO.

Blix looked on a moment, then reached out,
pinched a half-inch, stuffed it in his lower lip, said an
awkward "Thank you" and we rolled away.

Dora giggled through the first hundred yards.

I had stopped guessing *why*—the source of the
power of her unannounced swings from woe to mirth.
Now that I knew she could not harm *me*—being worse
off than I—I could witness her presence with nothing
worse than boredom. But after ten or so silent miles—
the heater working beautifully, Mae Clain's odor tam-
ing—I wondered what we *were*, what this truckload
constituted in the eye of God (or a thoughtful on-
looker, possessed of the facts)? A Ship of Fools? Blind
Leading the Blind? Wise and Foolish Virgins? Try it
another way—who would be the ideal painter to paint
us? Goya? (does one of us possess the dignity, the
unworked stillness, to bathe the others in his idiot
light?). Brueghel, surely. We are all lean enough. But
what would Brueghel call it, what would be his allegory?—four drunk Indian men, one pregnant drunk
squaw (all huddled in cold wind on the springs of a
truck—the passengers) and we up front, the steerers
(two sick Indian women, both abandoned by men; Blix
and I). Name us, name us!

We were in the hideous heart of Gallup (stan-
dard-American hideous—gas stations, burger stands,
cat's-cradles of wires, slush in gutters; its one unique
feature, on every corner as invariable furniture or like
berserk Christmas decorations, a Navajo couple, drunk,

in velveteen, gorgeous silver and turquoise, haranguing each other in the hoarse voice of hatred—wide mouths, clenched fists); and I still couldn't think what we were or where headed—*The Lame Entering First?* but entering what?

We had turned south by then—HOSPITAL ONE MILE—when the old woman jerked forward, slapped the dashboard and croaked in Navajo.

We were moving slowly—through small gray houses packed onto low hills—but Blix slowed more and asked Dora "What's wrong?"

"She say stop."

Blix pulled to the curb and stopped, looking forward.

The woman was struggling to rise now—clawing at Dora, the dashboard, the seat, to exit on my side.

Dora sat still, as though a cat were playing.

Blix said, "Do me a favor—see what in God's name's happening."

Still not moving, not touching the woman, Dora said a short sentence.

The woman let out a long ululation—a single syllable in the pit of her throat, surely no word—and again strained to stand.

Dora was silent.

Blix turned, laid one hand on the woman's shoulder and said through clenched teeth, "Help out, for Christ's sake."

Dora faced him and smiled. "What you need me for?"

"I can't turn her out here in the road. She'll die. What the Hell is she after?"

Dora said, "She say she got a daughter lives here.

She's going there now."

"Where, here on this street?"

Dora said another sentence.

The woman groaned again.

Blix said "I'm helping *you*."

Dora said, "You can't stop her. She know what she wants."

I knew Dora was right and reached for my doorhandle to climb down and help the woman leave.

Blix said to me "Sit still."

"She's old enough to vote," I said.

"Oh Jesus," Blix said.

He had worked, I noticed, through the names of deity in an interesting order, impersonal to personal—*God* to *Christ* to *Jesus*. He was in personal need.

He was looking now at me—first time in an hour—"Mr. Scorch," he said. "Everything scorches in your little wake."

"Or *stiffens*," I said.

"Or bleeds."

"This woman's got nothing but rheumatism; that's not mortal."

"Try to understand. I work here. I'm responsible. I told Dora's father I'd leave her with a doctor."

"Then do it," I said. "She won't jump out. Do it by all means if it's for old Cochise, your friend at last, your chewing-tobacco pal." I opened my door and slid down to the road.

The old woman crawled over Dora in an instant and, in two steps, joined me—or passed me, briskly, in her own direction.

Until then, I hadn't thought my way beyond freeing her; but the sight of her now—small and boned

like a bird, consuming her freedom like a trail of suet
laid suddenly before her—suggested again the simple
solution: *Leave; there are things you can spare yourself,
you owe him nothing.* I had turned her way, back away
from the truck, and reached the tailgate (heading
where? *away*) when Blix met me head-on, arriving from
his side—and as two of the drunk men climbed out and
strode off.

Blix halted among his collapsing duties and said
"*Wait please*" toward the farthest gone, the woman
and the drunks.

The two men stopped, faced round; but the
woman never paused. (At the sight of Blix—dry-faced
and pale—I'd been the first to wait.)

He watched the woman for a moment, then abandoned her—what did it cost him? with what could he
pay and whom? pay *whom?* He said to the men, "Are
you helping us or not?"

One of them took a few steps nearer. "We going
to get my radio."

Blix said "I can't wait."

The man considered, nodded.

"How'll you get home?"

He pointed high, the way we were headed. "That
ain't my home," he said and they left.

Blix looked then to me and slapped his flanks in
desperation. "—Mine neither," he said and smiled.

The drunk pregnant girl had one leg out the tailgate, struggling down.

I pointed Blix to look and he took it by the ankle
and firmly shoved her back—not a word. The skin of
her thin leg had dried till it took his gesture like a slate
—as she fell back howling, I could see he had written

on her skin with his nail, a zagging white line, impossible to read. Blix scrubbed his hand.

I said "What's it mean?" and pointed to her marked leg, out of sight in the truck.

Blix had not seen it. "Look. I'm fighting," he said, "not explaining human life."

"Fighting what?"

"To draw breath one more hour and unstick a truck worth two hundred dollars that may not be *there* when we get there."

I *bonged* like a fight-bell, to start his next round.

He scrambled for the cab.

I followed, on my side—to keep the girl inside and on her way home (was it her home? was her husband one of those that had gone for the radio?); to preserve Blix's sense of donating help; changing lives; to avoid solitude. Those were reasons I gave myself anyhow as we drove on south toward Dora's truck and whosever home.

A mile from town, houses thinned, all but vanished for miles. We might have been rammed down some time funnel to Judaea, first century—sudden small hills, tan and gray, clumped with low growth (pinyon, sage, juniper), still scattered with snow that had lasted the day and a few lambs scrounging. If I'd seen on my right, in the gap between hills, thirteen shaggy men in dirty robes, wet sandals, with cold horny feet, trudging up with staves for an afternoon rest-and-homily, I'd have thought it only right—as natural, as naturally *produced* by the place, as the dark kids (Navajo? Mexican?) who'd begun appearing now, home from school, along the road, checking rusty mail boxes set a tenth of a mile before tarpaper shacks, occasional hogans. Two Indian boys, eight and nine, were being

met as they walked up a gully toward their hogan by a
brother, age four or five, grim as Polyneices with a
plastic bow and arrow aimed at their hearts. All among
litter. Now that dwellings had begun again, however
sparsely, the hills showed litter wherever snow had
melted. Nothing native or exotic, nothing blessedly
organic that would silently rot but good immortal
American litter—fuchsia hairspray cans, wine bottles,
white plastic jugs that will outlast Mount Rushmore.
All as clear in this light, as equally *near*, as in noon-
drenched Di Chiricos or prisoners under question.

Odd, I thought—the sun was low now, coming
from my side—four-thirty, five—and the light was thin
and watery. Thin as the air—that would be it; the thin-
ness yielded clarity. Objects hurtled freely toward me
through the thinning air, their images at least. We were
rapidly climbing. My lungs and my heart seemed suddenly to have new floors, half higher than usual. I'd try
for deep breaths, the release of a yawn (I'd slept very
little); but depths were not there. I was breathing all
right—with Blix and Dora by me, still no sense of short-
age—but I felt like a castaway, living on his muscle, no
fat, no reserve, hands-on-ledge department. To comfort
myself and to show I'd survived our confrontation, I
asked Blix "What's our altitude?"

"No idea," he said.

"Do you?" I said to Dora.

She shook her head. "I don't live here."

Blix said "Your grandma does."

"Yep. I hadn't been up here since I was young."

Blix chose to make it some sort of last straw. Facing the road, he clenched his teeth and showed them;
then he said "Why?"

Dora looked to him but didn't answer.

I wondered if, again, some taboo were involved (Navajo men mustn't see their mothers-in-law; may children see their grandmothers?) and I watched Dora closely.

She was neither tense nor smiling—no signal yet of outburst. Her face (the quarter I could clearly see) was an image of patient curiosity—*why ask that of me? why be who you are?* She couldn't turn Blix.

Still not looking, he said "You speak English?"

She nodded Yes.

"Then I asked you a question."

Patience again, but twitches of baffled apprehension now.

"How come you've never been up here to your grandma's but are making me go?"

"You're helping me," she said.

"—In strange territory, with mud waistdeep, that you've never seen before?"

"I never wanted to see it."

Blix considered, took nearly a minute. "Maybe you'll get your wish. Maybe we'll never get there. Or if we do, maybe you'll just see it this once."

Dora understood what I'd already refused to believe he meant. She said "You think I'm dying."

He'd had time for regret, hadn't meant her to read him so thoroughly. "You told me what the doctors said."

"And you think that's true? You think they know? They *don't* know—because I never did tell them."

Blix said "Tell them what?"—his pressure leaking.

"—What's wrong with me, the reason my arms go dead and I faint."

He said "Tell me."

"A snake. I touched it."

Blix and I smiled simultaneously.

She struck his shoulder with her clenched right hand. "You listen. It's the truth. When I went to school, about eight years ago, we had this teacher—a man named Simmons—and everybody say they're scared of snakes. So one day he come into school with a snake—live and moving—and all the other kids, they jump back scared. But he say, 'No, it won't hurt nobody but rats and prairie dogs'; and he say ain't nobody brave enough to touch him? So I say yes. All the other kids yelling at me—'Don't touch no snake!' But I been brave so I walk up and he hold it out between his hands, and I rub it one time. Then he say to me 'Hold it,' and he hand it to me, so I take it and hold it. It's so strong in my hands, I can feel it living but I never been scared. Everybody else real quiet now. It was real dry. Then I hand him back and I go sit down. Everybody tell me, coming home, that I'll get sick and I'm still not scared. But I got sick. You know how?—like now, fainting, falling down, my arms going dead. I was real bad sick and nobody knew why since I wouldn't tell them; but my mama get a man and he come and sing all night and all day and—you know what?—I don't tell him neither, but he pull a snake right out of my arm. That morning. And I was better. That's all that's wrong with me."

She had transformed, telling it—from her prior sealed silly petulant self to something not larger but harder, lighter, radiating faith in the simple lies that would not slow her death. She looked on at Blix's profile a silent moment, then faced the road.

He said, "Well, I'm glad. Glad you know." No irony, no pity.

He's abandoned her, was what I knew next. *He's*

left her to die—her face ten inches from him, her thigh
touching his; she's farther away than if he'd never
come, never borrowed her narrow but deep resources.
So I took her part—again, remember. My whole addled
heart flowed across to her now. She was not of course
looking. I saw her as the lady in Dickinson's poem—

> *Because I could not stop for Death—*
> *He kindly stopped for me—*

and merely to companion her, this moment on her trip,
I said (aloud, calmly), "Here's all that's wrong with
me."

Blix was first to turn—long enough to swerve the
truck; I could hear our drunks tumbling.

Dora listened, not turning.

I knew she listened. I said it for her. "I am left
alone because I wanted to be."

She still didn't turn. She had not understood.

Neither had Blix but he wouldn't rest in that. He
said, "Did you really want it badly as that?"

Dora looked on at her own hands, flat on her
flanks, and began to move her fingers as though playing
some tune, some instrument. Random, atonal—her
own "Sugartime"?

The clear revelation, as though her hands made
signals—that not only did she not follow me or Blix
but was already bored and had lapsed into music not
misery—came to me as comic, exhilarating. After years
apart, after life-between-the-eyes, still we were talking
like college roommates—or (better) like ladies in late-
Henry James, hieratic, oracular, lethally threatening,
playing slow holy tennis in their heavy silent skirts.
And that quick vision produced another—or a feeling

not a picture. The ballooning of pleasure in my belly, chest, throat—astounding (in *me*, after these weeks, months) as grace descending on me in the beak of a dove. No sense of its cause or source till I spoke—my answer to Blix produced as the crest of the rise reached my lips—"Yes, what I wanted." I had not known that. But finding it now and saying it aloud—in a snow-covered desert with dusk coming on, to a truckload of cripples—I looked again to Dora, in hopes that she still would not understand.

Her fingers played on, a little slower than before and her eyes watched them. If she'd followed a word of what was said or meant, it had done nothing to her. Surely she'd heard—seen!—every day speeches, acts, that would shrink my pleasure to tepid tameness.

It was Blix I had struck. I could see it in his side face—tight again, bluish—though the truck required his energy just then. Having come maybe twenty miles south of Gallup on the narrow paved road, he was turning right now—at Dora's signal—onto what seemed a ten-foot-wide dirt track, deeper in mud than the one to Atso's.

I thought at once of boyhood newsreels—the Second War, halftracks mired to the axles in French or German mud, bone-tired dogfaces sunk to the calves in its loud cold clasp.

Blix had turned too fast and, in the first few yards, had to jockey furiously to hold us in the road—the single set of ruts from the last mad truck that seemed our only hope of continuing. But when he'd saved us from ditching and slowed to a crawl and shifted into four-wheel drive, he could speak—he'd saved it for us through his little crisis—"What's wrong with me—why

I'm in this fix, where I'm here today in mud thick as shit—is I can't believe there are people like you."

I said, "Is your pronoun singular or plural?"

He said "Meaning what?"

"—Meaning me alone, as a single monster, or Dora and me?"

He drove a little more—or his hands rode the wheel; the truck seemed safely locked in its ruts. Then he said "Plural."

"There are," I said. "Touch us and see." I held out my hand, palm down, across Dora. Rough as the ride was, it hung there steady.

He had the guts to do it—the stagey guts. He let me wait suspended as his free hand moved to Dora's arm (but cloth not skin); then he moved for mine and, watching the road, covered and pressed it with his own strong fingers as though really confirming.

He held for so long that I felt how much colder he was than I, felt my warmth passing toward him, and rolled from his grip. I said, "Careful, but I feel my power leave me."

"Jesus," he said and before I could wonder (was he joining my joke—one more rally in our match—or was he further appalled?), he had lost control (or obeyed the track and the Great Sky-Pilot) and sunk us in the ditch. We were listing heavily leftward, unsavable clearly; but he gunned the gas in a try to blast us free. The drunks were bobbling like empty hogsheads. Only when we'd plowed twenty yards up the ditch—deeper each yard—did he stop, kill the engine and sit a moment, silent.

Dora and I were also silent, as though at the shrine to a fallen hero. I thought one thing—"I didn't buy boots; I am in suede shoes."

Then Blix said "Beg my pardon."

I thought he'd slipped, had meant to beg ours so I said "Of course."

"No, do, please," he said. He lowered his head almost to the wheel.

Dora looked to me and nodded in confirmation— we were back on ground she could recognize.

"I am Prince of Darkness, then," I said. "Now you know. Don't hold it against me."

Blix shook his head. "I do."

But by then the drunks were bailing out in back; their girl was wailing.

I turned, before Blix, and could see the two men already on the ground, the girl starting down. "We're ditching our ballast anyhow," I said.

Blix didn't answer but opened his door and stood on the little ledge and said to the men "Just wait." Then he leapt far out, across the ditch to the low snowy shoulder and looked down from there at the truck, the buried wheels, not at me or Dora (now the least of his problems).

Dora turned to him though and slid into his place behind the wheel.

I said to the back of her head "What now?"

She looked back quickly and gave a short giggle, her first for hours. Then she slid across the seat to Blix's door and—with no hesitation, barely looking as she went—she jumped up toward him and landed in soft snow; her sneakers sank to the ankles at once.

My being the monster permitted me to hold my own inside, warm and dry anyhow, till word to abandon ship. I did lean across and say to Blix, "I'll drive if you'll push."

He took it calmly—someone would have to drive;

someone had volunteered—and nodded, not looking. Then he said to Dora, "Whoever they are, tell the girl just to wait."

Dora said "She won't listen."

Blix said, "Tell her anyhow; then they can't blame me."

Dora shrugged and went.

Then one of the men, the smallest, came up, mud already to his knees, and said "You ain't going to move."

Blix took it as offered, as fact, delivered calmly, disaster number so-and-so; and he clearly believed it. But he said, "Yes I am. I got chains in back."

"How you going to put them on?"

Blix said, "On my hands and knees in the mud" and walked back to start.

I suddenly thought, "I am at their mercy. Again I have volunteered to be at the mercy of incompetents who can harm me, ruin me. Why? Blix asked me 'What next?' and has made me see the answer—to be free in my own life, free *not* to volunteer for work I neither need nor want, free not to yield again to Love the Great Occupation, Time-Passer, Killer. Free to say 'So what?' to everything but food and air. Yet now he has wrecked me in a desert mudhole with night coming down, the air cold and thin, my only hope for rescue three drunk Indians, one that's turning to stone and a social worker with his head up his ass about six light-years." I knew of course there was no real danger. We were hardly more than two miles off the highway. If we were firmly stuck, if worse came to worse, we could simply walk out and hitch a lift to Gallup and thence, by bus, to Dunder (and my rented car, and home)—

providing the Indians stayed drunk and docile, didn't
kill us for our cash. But what then? what next?—once
home and free? At that, I felt as precious as uranium,
made of energy, each cell an atom that could radiate,
steady and generous, for years without visible exhaustion—the radiance of simple knowledge; of what *I*
know, having had my life; the wasteless conversion of
mass into power. Power for what?—further life and
freedom. So I sat, a little huddled round myself as
round a glow, while the truck rocked gently with shoulders from beneath and voices came to me in Navajo
and English, exasperated, stripped of the upholstery of
kindness—"Stand there, goddammit . . . Hold this,
goddammit . . . Why dontcha put it here?" We were
now, I thought, *The Drones and the Mate*—I the
consort chosen (for *qualities*) and groomed for union,
toward which I am borne through dangers and trials.
Union with what?—that new life and work, my fresh
rich chance, clear hope, ahead. If they rescue me now,
award me survival.

Blix jumped to the shoulder again, at my left—a
mudbaby, frowning.

I slid a little over and lowered the glass.

He said, "Please crank it now and drive it slowly
out."

"Why don't you?" I said.

"You'll need me back here—need all three of us
pushing."

I looked back at Dora and the one man in mud,
then quickly through the window into the cab—the girl
and the second man unconscious, flat-out. I'd need Blix
there, as he'd said, so I nodded.

"Drive slow and straight," he said, "till the ditch

goes shallow; then gun it out into the center ruts and
keep moving slow. We'll have to jump on."

I cranked, shifted gear, waited till Blix yelled
"OK" from the back, then released the clutch slowly.
The wheels spun once; then the chains gripped somehow and—heaved by three shoulders—I moved straight
forward at my leftward-listing angle for maybe ten
yards till the ditch, instead of shallowing, deepened. Or
the mud did. I still moved, but slower; the list was
increasing with every yard, the left wheels sinking. I'd
gone twenty yards and I wanted to stop—I was wreck-
ing us deeper than we'd been before; an axle would
break—and I did raise my foot from the gas an instant.

But Blix yelled *"Go!"*

So I floored it and went, wallowing grandly—the
drunk girl, the girl!—and the truck saved itself. Or
saved me maybe. The ditch never shallowed but,
slowly, the wheels were grinding rightward; and I was
borne out and up, across to the haven of the center ruts
—Blix still close behind me, still yelling "Move!"

I moved a little faster, feeling the sudden need to
leave—leave the three rescuers, filthy, in my wake and
flounder ahead (with my two oblivious drunks). Toward what though? So I slowed and, seeing I had
reached a short level stretch at the crest of a rise, I
stopped and waited.

First to reach me was the man. Embarrassed by his
speed, he looked back to Blix and laughed and said,
"Him! You ought to hire him. He'll get us there." (I
could hear Dora giggle.) Then he gave me a fumbling
army salute, said "Pretty good all right!" and vanished
toward the rear.

Blix appeared and stood two steps away, looking.

He of course said "Jesus." Then "Hand me that towel."

I was still at the wheel, giddy from success and vision and the height; but I looked to the floor and saw a wadded towel. "It's dirtier than you," I said.

"Most things are."

"I advise against it, Doc. Barely sterile," I said.

"Me neither," he said. "But *you'll* sterilize it. Just touch it once for me."

I took it up, held it a moment before me—Blix made a sizzling sound—then threw it out to him.

Dora had come up and waited separate from Blix, but watching him. My wheels had spun mud into her face and hair; but—unlike Blix whose hands hung isolated beside him, untouchable—she seemed not to mind. Her hands touched her skirt. And she was breathing as though the air were sufficient, calm and thick. As though she were home, despite her denials.

Blix scrubbed at his hands and wrists—his face was clean—then handed the towel to Dora and said to me "You did it."

"Black magic," I said. "It was nothing, just my Powers."

He stepped toward me, not looking back to Dora, and said, "My thanks. Now see can your Powers get us all the way there, wherever *there* is."

I didn't want to yield my grip on the wheel; but Blix had a foot on the running board already, scraping off mud. I hadn't moved. Dora came to her door and climbed and entered.

Blix said "You want to drive?"

I could not imagine riding a mile *between* them. I smiled and said "You trust me?"

"No," he said and smiled. "But I don't trust anybody else who's with us either."

"Not yourself?" I said.

"Oh, *me*, yes," he said. But by now he was lit with something like glee. Cold, wet and stiffening with mud, he looked up to me once more from the ground and said, "No, you do it. Magic, magic—" He flung out his arms in a wizard posture, his hands clawed downward, eyes blared, laughing.

"How far do we go?" I said.

"Ask Dora," he said.

She said "About two mile."

Blix held his fading pose—"You've never been here."

Dora said "I know."

Blix said, "Two miles may mean twenty but— magic! magic! We're charmed, we're saved." And before I could think—accept or decline—he'd trotted through sucking mud to the passenger side and taken my old seat.

So I drove us on—nothing else to do; I could not fold now—and after a hundred yards, I was glad. The steering demanded every quantum of my energy—time, eyes, mind. (The truck would hold the road calmly for yards, in the ruts as on rails; then—no warning—the wheel would lurch in my hands and I'd save us again. Blix and Dora understood and barely spoke.) And after all, I was piloting at last—not ideally, not alone (with all this breathing cargo) but at least at nobody's mercy but my own (and the engine's, the snow and mud's, the night's).

For instantly, it was night—the air too thin to hold light or color once the sun had sunk. In my concentration, I'd hardly noticed and pressed toward the glass to see the road.

Finally Blix said "Light has been invented."

I looked over to him for clarification and the truck slewed badly; I fought it into line.

"Your *headlights*," he said.

I said "I can see."

"It's my truck," he said.

"It's Uncle Sam's," I said, *"ergo* mine as much as yours." But I switched on the lights and wallowed ahead at an unsteady ten or so miles an hour. Through pure intensity of searching, I saw in my first slow mile a single house set far back on our right (not a hogan— logs?), no trace of light but the voices of dogs above our roar; then nothing again, then a '49 Buick abandoned, maroon (its lovely slave-bracelet hood-ornament intact!); then nearer the road on my left a sheepfold built carefully of wood (where was all this wood *found?*) but abandoned too, collapsing, not a sheep in sight. All this time the road was struggling to halt us, expel us, ditch us—short flat stretches of a hundred yards or so that (though the mud was deep) raised our hearts (all three; I could taste that in the air—hope! we'd *continue!*); then a sudden bucking of steep hills, deep drops. I thought, at the top of every hill (they were steeper and steeper), that we'd see Dora's truck; but half an hour later (five miles farther in) we were still moving on through emptiness. Not exactly desolation—the Dead Sea, Death Valley, are no doubt sparser —but this road, the few feet of shoulder we could see (barbed wire, short old-style power poles, then sage again and pinyon), was competing handsomely. I thought of Auden's stanza from "The Shield of Achilles"—

reverse alone through eight miles of mud. But I was not
responsible. The trap was not mine—not chosen by me,
not self-deployed (except insofar as I'd meant this trip
to be a change, relief, light-entertainment among the
more seriously deprived than I)—and clearly I was safe.
At the worst, a night in Grandma's hogan (a few fleas,
chilly, the sounds of family-humping); at best, an exhilarating triumph over mud (a tricky turn-round, then
the trip back out—surely faster now, three Indians
lighter, the mud chilling and thickening).

Blix turned and came toward me, opened my door,
climbed up.

I stayed in place, behind the wheel.

"Slip over," he said.

"You still don't trust me?"

"No."

I didn't move.

"Please," he said. "I have got to try and drive us
around this wreck."

I moved, he sat, I said "What's beyond it?"

"Grandma's, I'm *assuming*. I'm assuming somehow we can stay there till morning or turn and come
back."

"She won't have you," I said.

"You know her?"

"No. Do you?"

"Never saw her," he said. "Can't read her mind
either." He shifted gear downwards.

"I can," I said. "She'll hate your sight."

He actually waited. He shifted into neutral, faced
me and said "Why?"

I was looking ahead. No Indian-Bureau expert
could have separated Dora more effectively from her

drunk—what? kin?—than our white headlights. In their glare, ahead, huddled at the wreck, she had crossed back over—to my eye at least—and hung there by the others (not *with* them though) as oblivious to us as a fetus to its mother. Not true exactly. They all were fetal now—pale, lunar in our light, but with simple needs only, which their element supplied (the thin air, the muck), not in need of us. Cruel to addict them. I answered Blix, "Because you've ruined Dora."

He nodded. "Check," still hung-fire, not moving.

"Leave then," I said.

"Now?"—his tone considered it as possible, not preposterous.

"The kind thing," I said.

"How?" Blix said.

"Is this a through road?"

"Who knows?" he said.

"—We won't till we try."

"What if it dead-ends at Grandma's hogan?"

"That'll be round," I said. "We can circle it."

"We'd meet her coming back—Dora, we'd meet."

"She'd have got the message by then," I said.

"What would it say?"

I thought. "It would say, 'It is a far far better thing—' "

"That would be from you," he said. "What would *my* message be?"

I said "Write it yourself then." I was tired of the game and thought for the first time since dark of the vista spy. I could play *him* now, an invincible trump.

But Blix said, "Oh I have. Many times in many tongues." He was of course looking ahead to where she stood, talked at by her kin, silent herself but not turn-

Chinese sages in a late Yeats poem. Helpless idiots.

Only Dora was silent but she listened.

There were clumps of stunted trees a few yards away. I went to them and took an armload of sticks. The four minutes' effort had me sweating lightly and breathing fast—I thought more of the warmth than the altitude: good, tonight would be warmer than last night at least; Grandma's might even be bearable. The sky showed the reason—low thick clouds, the day's warmth trapped on us; we were under a bell; pray it didn't lift.

When I got back to the truck—my shoes still barely damp—Blix was up in the cab. Dora, the girl and the happy drunk were bracing themselves to push from the rear. Only the other man—too dazed to push? —was standing aside.

He watched me coming with my load of brush, really studied me; then when I stopped near him, poised to hand it down to Dora (who was nearest the stuck wheel), he had reached his conclusion, drained my meaning. He even came to me—three or four steps —touched my loaded arms, shook his head No and said, "You ain't gonna start no fire with that."

Fire had been the furthest thing from my mind, but I had to ask "Why?" He'd threatened an irrational prohibition and I wasn't welcoming those.

His head shook on, a mime of negation—"We ain't got no matches."

I laughed but he didn't. He was in dead-earnest (and right, as it turned out—not a match among us; how did he know?). So for racial harmony, I tried to stop. I managed a solemn nod—still more loaded with sticks than anyone in Grimm—then surrendered to the spectacle of me marooned (maybe) with four redskins in snow and mud at roughly 7,000 feet and not one of us with the simple knowledge of how to nurse fire.

Before I'd decided to sacrifice my shoes and join the pushers, Blix made his first try at driving out, a forward-backward-forward struggle that left the four Indians stuccoed with mud—Dora in sneakers—and the wheel buried deeper, and sinking fast. In a moment of waiting, it settled six inches—was it in quicksand? or (far more likely, considering the day) in some small spot where the earth lacked a crust, some tunnel to the center? Entrance to the afterworld, a four-day journey.

Blix shouted something then from the cab, and I assumed he would make a second try and that pushing was more good to him than sticks; so I dropped my bundle and said to the drunk, "No, but come on; we can push." Then I stepped past him to jump for the ditch.

But the other drunk—the helpful one, pushing—said "No! Stay there."

I thought he meant his friend so I kept climbing down.

But he said again "No."

I stopped and said "Me?"—my feet still clean; only my hands were wet.

The man didn't answer but held out both arms toward me. It seemed the gesture of father to child—*Jump, I'll catch you*—and I took another downward step.

But a woman said "No."

I looked—Dora surely; she was facing me; the drunk girl was yards away, leaning on the far wheel (wretching or pushing?).

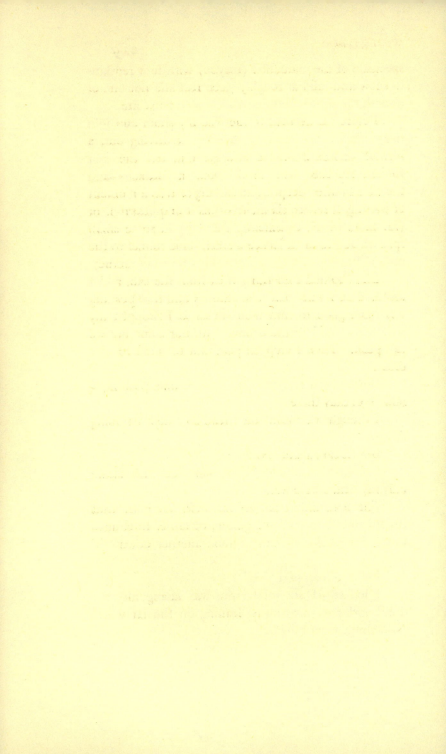

Blix said "What are *you* about?"

"I asked first—what's the powwow?"

"Who knows? Just think of it as Mystery-of-the-Minute. There'll be millions more before day—and day may get here before they finish talking."

They did seem Biblical now or T. E. Lawrencian, no longer sage and calm—a small knot of shepherds locked in suddenly urgent hassle over some microscopically trivial issue, beneath the sky and the wheeling constellations.

After Dora's first statement, the helpful drunk talked most—with raucous lunges from the pregnant girl, now hoarse from wretching.

Blix simply stood, showed no inclination to climb out of mud to the shoulder with me; so I said "Why this honor?"

"Meaning what?"

"—Letting me choose our fate—the stranger in your midst."

He hadn't thought but he said at once "I'm tired."

"I didn't sleep either—different reason, remember? And we clearly won't tonight, whatever she decides."

"No," he said.

"I could transport us psychokinetically to a motel in Gallup—hot showers, blankets; ready?" I extended wizard arms, as he had earlier.

"That's why," Blix said, "—why I told you to choose, not your magic games but your cool clear head. Frozen—Birdseye Brains."

"Meaning what please?"

"You know," he said, "—know I think you're a monster."

"What kind please?"

"There's only one—the killing kind."

"Her?"

"Yep. You know it."

"Not true," I said.

"Oh don't get me wrong; I admire you," he said, "—envy you your powers, all but worship you." He bowed, where he stood, deeply from the waist; his right hand touched the mud.

"Don't," I said.

"I'm just a man," he said.

And Dora started back toward us. She came to Blix, stopped four feet away and said "We better walk."

"On to your grandma's?"

"Back home," she said.

"Dunder?—that home?"

"Yep."

"Which way?"

"Back the way we come."

Blix said, "That's miles—eight, nine—just to the highway. By the time we get there, we'll never catch a ride—it's not Times Square."

"We can't walk that other way," she said and again pointed my way, but still not looking.

"Why?"

"Maybe too dark."

"Can't one of them lead us?—they walked it this morning."

"Nope," she said.

"He's sober by now." Blix meant the helpful drunk.

"No he ain't," she said.

I knew, whatever happened, I was in for mud and

time and then—Labrador!"

"Do you know where we are?"

He pointed to the truck. "I checked a map. Are
you ready?—Remnant Mesa, just south of Remnant
Mesa. 'A remnant shall remain.' "

"*Who?*" I asked.

He turned to Dora. "Who are you going with?"

Had she decided? Was it automatic yet? She
waited ten seconds, looking at the dark ground. "You
and him," she said.

So I was included. Odd—why? To show she didn't
fear me? didn't countenance my powers or my haunted-
ness? Or maybe that she *did*—ranked me with her
snake as a cause of woe—but was tolerating me as a
necessary adjunct to her time with Blix? One more
landmine in the field she must walk. I asked what Blix
wouldn't—"Do they know? Do they mind?"

She nodded to me. "I tell them." But she kept her
place.

Blix at last said, "You'll *tell* them or you've *told*
them already?"

"Yep," she said. "Already."

We both—Blix and I—looked toward them then.

They were still in the dark at the front of Dora's
truck, twenty feet away, between us and the road. They
stood close and silent; even the girl had recovered and
stood straight and still, her blanket tight round her.

Blix said "Where are they going?"

"I don't know," she said. "They live round here."

Blix said "Why are they waiting?"

She only shrugged.

I laughed and said, "Do they ever kill witches?"

Dora said "Yep."

Blix said "At intervals." Then he asked Dora, "Anything else to tell them?"

"I ain't talking to them."

"We're off then," Blix said and took the first step. The drunks stood in place.

"Blix. Wait," I said. Oddly, I'd thought of the trucks—no one else had seemed to.

He and Dora stopped, looked back.

"What about all this hardware?"

"It'll wait," Blix said. "There's a motorpool in Gallup. They'll tow mine in."

"Dora's?"

"It's OK." she said. They started again.

"We're blocking traffic," I said.

"Whiz, whiz," Blix said. "Walk-to-left-facing-traf-fic." His next three steps were a bobbing-weaving dance as he threaded Broadway.

The helpful drunk stepped forward from his group.

"You're fired," I said.

Blix didn't turn; Dora followed him.

"Blix, you were fired this afternoon. The VISTA spy turns out to have teeth."

That stopped him, turned him. He walked three steps back toward me, past Dora. "I forgot him."

"Yes, you did."

"He came by, did he?"

"—And got an eyeful. And left you a message."

"What was the eyeful?"

"Dora at her post—the bedroom door."

"What was the message?"

"Wait—he also got an earful."

"Who from?"

"Dora and me."

"What did *she* say?"

"That she lived there."

"You?"

"I sort of scared him—Leaves from My Life or The Bloody Wife."

We all were frozen still—Dora, the helpful drunk, the silent others.

Blix said "And the message?"

"To phone him collect by noon tomorrow."

"For what?"

"He said you'd know, said you'd know what's coming."

Dora had waited where she'd stopped, no nearer.

Blix looked back to her now—"Did he?"

"I guess so."

"He did," I said. "I don't tell real lies—not anymore. His name was Tim Neely—looked helpless, apparently isn't."

"No, he's not," Blix said. He stood a moment, facing me. Then he beckoned to me, with a kind of kitchen gesture (stirring soup)—"On to the nearest phone. Bitter pills." He turned and went.

Dora let him take the lead again, then fell in behind—four, five paces. In a second they had flanked, then passed, her kin—who did not look after them but stared on at me.

I knew no more delays; my lines to Blix and Dora were lengthening with each step; I was nearer her kin than she. They could not so much as start a fire though. So I followed.

And they let me pass in silence—no muttered imprecations to meet my powers in dark midair, no visible gestures to turn my gaze, no movement, breaths held.

Scared as I was, I longed to rush at them with some Halloween groan—*Arrgh! It's I!*—but I only said "Thank you" to the helpful drunk and never broke step.

No need to compel you through the first hour's walking. You'd have nothing to do but play drill sergeant, counting cadence at my heels—unless you're a fight fan, which I am not. Ordeal (the actions of ordeal, its present-time) is invariably unrevealing to a witness, except of his own fragility and blood-lust, no news to most adults—Harold Lloyd on a ledge, fingernails in mortar, or Jesus crucified or Jacob and the man who wrestled all night. What's revealing there is not the grunt and groan—what holds were used and why, the man's dirty move in crippling Jacob's hip—but what was said at dawn, the words between the battlers ("Your new name is Israel" —"What is *your* name?") which flood the night backwards with terror and joy, the dirty winner having been God of course. So you and I will know, only at the end—and in my words— if the trip was worth joining. Not that I had a choice; the choice was to die.

There were no sights to see—with the cloud-cover holding, thank God, no moon; and we walked in near blackness on the right-hand shoulder where the snow had not melted and the ground was mostly level. No acts to study, for character or motive (or grace or *eros*) —foot following foot, silent breath on breath. No talk to hear—not a syllable from Dora, only rare relaxed questions from me ("How fast are we walking?") and Blix's replies ("Not fast enough"). No thoughts to overhear.

Not from me at least. I didn't think—my brain a ball of cheese. Oh no doubt the ancient cellar lobes were grunting intermittently in their precious perpetual night; but mostly they were doing their oldest intended work—answering alarms, directing each nerve and muscle onward through snow toward warmth, dryness, food; and doing it with pathetic spaniel eagerness (being so seldom called upon, my life being largely safe as a stone).

Till now. Safe till now. And in that first hour I felt more than safe—exhilarated, simply triumphant. I had won, would win. Won what?—freedom, competence. Two hours ago, I'd felt fragile as glass, rocked round in mud by the hands of drunk Indians. Now the sense of *fragility* had changed to *value* and *worthiness*, plus the new-proved power to protect that value. I remembered my father once saying of my mother, "She's fragile as a lamp-chimney but stand me behind her when the A-bombs fall." I felt that now—a fine lamp-chimney that's survived Hiroshima. Entirely undisturbed. Adamantine, in fact.

Felt it though, as I said, not *thought* it. I was near as I've been since, say, age eleven to a state of pure being—the mind of God. I speak for myself of course, not the others. They were moving like me (Blix leading, Dora between us); we were even in step three-fourths of that hour; but what they were thinking or feeling or suffering, I didn't guess or care. Not in the first hour.

But soon after that, the charm began to fade. No

sudden vanishing, no emergency bells, no change of weather or scenery. But my lower brain, for its own slow reasons, began to suspect it knew more than my upper—that it wasn't merely chuffing me along through a lark, my first winter-carnival, but was straining to ram me through danger to safety (or ram itself through; *I* was mainly its luggage). After the hour of surprise that my lounge-lizard's get-up was perfect kit for a forced march through desert snow—I had walked warm and dry—I began to feel stripped. Not instantly but slowly, and from the ground up. My feet, in suede, were finally ice; my scrotum was coarsening, tightening at its base like draw-strung marble-bags in my child-hood; and my heart, warm till now in its Harris-tweed jacket, lurched into fast-time to flush down warm blood. And in its new rhythm, the coded message any fool could read: *It is possible to die. Here. Soon.*

My first thought was defiance—"I refuse to die here, a foreign death, out of my element. I must fight to die *in place*, to die where I should (which is where? where?) not in some stray ditch, erroneous, muffled—Jesus in the sink of the Colosseum, not on high Gol-gotha; Cleopatra frigid in the mistletoe of Gaul; or the first man to die on Mars or Uranus. Will he have time to notice (or sufficient emotion?—will that have been trained-out?) that he suffocates in scenery which he cannot even use for metaphor, much less life? He won't know the name of the rock he falls on. My wife on the tiles—to spare the rugs, upholstery. Me near Remnant Mesa. The answer is No."

By now the road had begun to rise and fall—hard climbs, steep drops—and the warmth of day, despite clouds, was rising. No remnant would remain. The ground beneath the snow was colder, the snow was thickening—not ice yet but poised. My feet were the ice.

Look. This is not my line of work at all, not the tune to which my faculties march. I may have to die of boredom, embarrassment—one more failed scout-master, draped on the rocks. I'm capable of spelling it out for you, in every increasingly pressurized moment —finding stripped howling language to compel your company every step of my way toward agony, physical and mental desperation; but you've read Jack London, you've seen Yukon movies (Preston Foster, Bruce Cabot—eyelashes frosted). May I leave it to you?— Chinese-opera scenery? You have all the elements; build it around me—the night, the struggle. It had started well, was getting bad, would clearly get worse unless an Army tank—nothing else could make it— should have left Gallup, say, three hours ago intent on nothing but our personalized rescue. *How much worse?* of course. That is all no more than the gears of melo-drama; do your work on the weather, the road condi-tions; leave me free to dissect the *action* for you.

After three or four hills and their drops, I was scared. Frost-bite, trench-foot, amputations, stumps. I called to Blix "Stop please."

He obeyed so quickly that Dora walked into him; and he not only stopped but, moving her gently aside, came toward me. He stood a moment, silent, a foot from my face.

I extended my left hand and gripped his shoulder (to steady myself to remove my left shoe and check for frost-bite).

He accepted, stood still but he said "What must I do?"

"You're doing it," I said. "Prop me up a minute while I saw off this foot."

He said, "No, I mean *me*. What must I do now?"

"Feel my foot and see if it's frozen yet."

"It's not," he said, not even looking down.

"Thanks, Doc," I said. "You learned a lot in four years."

"No, tell me," he said.

"*You're* the doctor," I said.

"*You're* the man that's made it—tell me what I must do. Now."

Massaging my wet foot—far warmer than my hand!—I tasted relief. I thought he meant *now*, our physical dilemma—how must he, our Volunteer-in-Service, serve us now? how dodge us past death? I was not alone then. So I said, half-whispering to spare Dora (*what?*), "Go back up front and put right foot after left for another six miles and pray through your teeth for the clouds to hold and the highway to be there where we left it, bumper-to-bumper traffic, hot soup and warm baths and eiderdown beds."

"No." He waited, bearing my weight. "No. After that—" as though that plain miracle were guaranteed, a matter of form, just round the next bend. I *was* alone.

"Wait till then," I said. "You may have me to ship east for burial, stiff as a popsicle, twice as sweet. That'll keep you busy, take your mind off yourself." I was done with my feet, I'd released his shoulder. My heart was still racing—the altitude—my breaths, even standing still, were little yips, love-breaths, ecstasy. I needed to move.

But Blix held ground. In full voice, to spare nobody, he said "Help me."

"Why me?" I said. I could just see Dora's back.

She was still faced forward, awaiting her leader, her sneakers well out of sight under snow.

"You're the only white man within twenty miles."

"Then hump your black ass, boy, and tote me *home*."

"You're my oldest friend."

I hummed three notes of *Hearts and Flowers*, as though blowing a comb. "Not good enough," I said.

"You've made it," he said.

"Made what?"

"Your way out."

"Out to where?" I said, "—Remnant Mesa by night, on hoof through snow?"

"Tell me how," he said.

I decided he meant it, was really *asking*. The truth seemed simple—"Because I wanted to."

"Not good enough," he said.

"Blix, I'm freezing. Lead me out and I'll plan your whole future—an entirely happy life, money-back guarantee."

Dora came toward us three steps and waited, facing Blix's back.

Meaning what? I wondered. *Is she audience or client or investigator for the prosecution?* I spoke past Blix to her—"Dora, tell him what to do."

"Stay back," Blix said but did not turn to her.

She said "OK" and retracted a step.

I said to Blix, "You're asking about her?—or is she already settled?"

"—Her," he said.

"Let *her* say then."

"She won't do that." He had spoken full voice from the start, no concealment. I'd accepted his lead.

"Let me ask her," I said.

"For yourself or me?"

"Oh Jesus—for *you*. All *my* questions were answered two weeks ago. You are facing a man who is Fully Informed."

"Liar," Blix said.

"Shall I ask her? She'll answer. They answer me."

He turned and faced her.

I remembered his chronic myopia—how much could he see? He could strike a match and test her. But then—O, Tara!—clouds broke on the moon. We were instantly blanched, our shadows pitched silently forward in snow.

She was watching him—watching, not searching or consuming or extracting.

Blix broke and turned to me. "Now you're in trouble. Clouds lifting. You'll freeze."

We all looked up and, as in some old DeMille Bible film, the dome had cracked. Our warming clouds were rapidly yawning on a sky like a gullet, black and bottomless. Where there had been only muzz and moisture, there were now fierce stars by the tens of thousands that seemed (for the first time in my experience) set, not in one plane of uniform distance (a Ptolemaic globe) but at infinitely variable heights and depths. Desert clarity. We seemed—all three, staring up, bathed with light—under desperate treatment, chosen for some titanic ray-therapy as last resort and pinned here now under massive bombardment. Dora's sclerosis. Blix's bad lung. My what? Or was it therapy? Perhaps annihilation? We were withering as we stood.

Blix said "We'd better move" and took steps to go.

He was passing Dora when I said "No. Listen."

"To what?" he said.

"My Last Words to Man." I sniffed once to show that I thought I was joking. "You'll never walk alone —but you sure as Hell can *run*." I expected more would follow but my mouth hung empty.

Blix said "Is that my answer?"

"Yep."

"Warm thanks."

"Make 'em hot," I said and stamped my dead feet.

He turned and took the lead again; we all trudged on.

Another hour, worse with every step—and we never paused, never spoke a syllable (breath was too scarce). In the first twenty minutes of open sky, the snow had frozen stiff—so suddenly that in memory it seems to *clank* shut at the instant of rigidity. Our wet feet labored now to break its crust; and since in any case the shoulder was narrowing (the barbed wire on our right had snagged me now twice; my jacket was ruining, shoes long since ruined), Blix led us down into the road—a lesser evil. The mud was still soft, warmer than the snow though it couldn't hold for long at the present rate of chilling. All wind had dropped. Nothing whatever could return the fleeing warmth—unless, by *fiat*, there should be another day, a sunrise tomorrow. Eight hours at least. We were utterly flayed. So was the desert, this half of the earth. Lidless, stripped. Nothing between us and entropy. Three running-down lives in a running-down world.

Maybe it had *run* down, the world, there—we the

last hold-outs, doomed but *here*. Another victory—I'd
have made it unaided to the absolute end (unless I
should drop now, before Blix and Dora) when she had
bailed-out with so little time to go, two bearable weeks.
I was thinking by now—or tasting, touching triumph. I
was bare of regrets as a six-weeks baby. I could see the
questions that would go unanswered as clearly as the
moon. Why did I want it? Simply because I had ceased
to need her? How had I come to that so soon? How
does it happen to a human being?—that after ten million years of herd-life, pair-life, he wants pure freedom,
the freedom of a child (not to yearn or lean), of a pri-
mal cell with no need to divide, no thought of conju-
gation, bathed in hot salt seas for the few days it has,
few hours, minutes? Unanswered and, now, unanswer-
able. By me at least. *I will not care.* I would die un-
puzzled, if nothing else. Not appeased, not pleased but
not defiant either and, now, not puzzled. A youngish
ox (who might have pulled his load) led lowing, not
bellowing, to the slaughter.

Oh I knew the world was there, where we'd left it
—the searchlight beacon from the Gallup airport
showed clearly now that the sky had lifted, a rising-
collapsing stroke of light on our left hand. Little Piper-
Cubs could be puttering in every minute now, hauling
what?—rich Indians to the Shalimar Motel? Steaks
huge enough to gorge every mouth and doggy-bagsful
for the wolves at the hogan, the children, Grandma;
warm rooms, hot water, warm beds.

But the light's place was rigid. It would not recede,
not fall behind us. When it first appeared—Blix
pointed it out, not speaking—I had welcomed it as a
buoy, a still point against which to judge our forward

progress; but now, much later, it was where it had been.
Was it following us, at precisely our speed? Or were we
not moving at all but on a treadmill, the earth sliding
beneath us, consuming our efforts? I would never arrive
to claim my reward, to say what I'd learned—how I'd
foiled her death, her punishment by the simple expe-
dient of desiring it, *requiring* it. So by her own lights—
motive and purpose—she has died in vain, her gunshot
as silent as an ice-crack at the pole. *No one there to
hear it.* Yet I did hear of course—not the shot itself
(I'd been ten miles away) and not at once but now its
fullest double meaning—her intent and mine; her ac-
complishment and mine. Now, could I ever tell it? To
tell it is to beat her at her own hateful game. I called
to Blix again—"Please stop!" My voice now was frail,
the sound as scary and disembodied as though it had
leaked from the power wire overhead that had been our
companion every step of the way, silent till now.

Didn't he hear or did he refuse? He didn't stop.

I knew I'd made noise at least—Dora glanced back
once but also kept moving.

I would overtake her, touch Blix direct. But I'd
need that strength for later—for worse than this. I
stopped in my tracks, let them gain a few steps; then I
called from that distance—"Blix, I'll answer you."

He took another three steps before he spoke, still
never stopping—"Too late. I know my own."

"Then tell me that."

They were twenty yards ahead now. "No use to
you," he said.

"Let *me* decide that."

No word. They walked on.

I would not catch up now. I would soon be alone.

"Wait, anyhow, please."

Blix said "We can't." His voice was unshaken by his stride, unfatigued. *He works here, he's at home.*

I knew that was his answer, reached since he'd asked me—that his *we* meant *them*, him and Dora. They would make it safely out, regardless of me, and pack their junk and leave tomorrow together, without her children, by bus from Gallup. Or stay and sink here, two more litter factories, their own home-industry, their lifetime's work—a mutual surrender: Blix to a simple need fillable elsewhere, under a roof at least, in a dry bed at least, where his own simpler language is understood and answered; Dora to a further more humiliating bondage than any laid on her by her people, their past life, her own short ugly life, her body gone mad now and crawling toward its death. Not crawling —striding. I needed to laugh but again gauged my breath and knew I must wait. What mattered was to catch them.

And in four minutes of agony, I did. (I'm speaking precisely; agony is accurate—the sense, with each step, of over-extension of every resource; my heart blundering wildly against chest and throat like a terrified child in a cell walled with paper from which air is draining; can the paper contain him as it crushes inward? can he tear through and breathe?) I reached out now and touched Dora not Blix. "Listen, please."

She stopped and turned and faced me, smiling.

My eyes, blurred and dancing, saw a moving light above her—a star, not falling but belting the sky, laterally, slowly. "Look there," I said.

It was not a tactic but it stopped Blix and held him. He followed my pointing finger, waited a moment. He was breathing calmly.

I said "What is it?"

Dora shook her head—did she see it at all? or a different sky entirely, wreathed with crippling reptiles picked out in light, or opening in tunnels on her new safer life that Blix had confirmed?

"A satellite," Blix said. "First one I've seen, even out here."

"—Watching *you*," I said. "Another VISTA spy."

"Good luck," he said up toward it.

Dora giggled and looked down to me. (The road sloped up; I was downhill from her, even three feet away.) "Watching you," she said.

"Why me?" I smiled too.

"You know," she said.

I did. It was what I had run to tell them. "I killed her."

Dora nodded, murder no doubt weekly news to her.

Blix stood in place, still watching the satellite, but said "What else is new?"

"I did," I said. "I'd know."

"You think you did," he said, "—like to think you did."

"I know—yes."

He looked down toward me then. (Was the satellite gone? I'd lost it anyhow.) "That's your answer," he said, "—that you stopped us for?"

"Yes."

"To what question please?"

I could not remember. I laughed and said "Help me."

"That was it," he said.

He had lost me entirely—fear of him stood up now with other fears: night, cold, exhaustion. Blix would be her avenger—she had written to him, Last Written Words. He bore her blessing to condemn, punish, abandon me here. It had been her plan; she had won after all. For the moment, I believed that—or it squatted on my chest and throat, a stifling weight, therefore surely a fact. But I said "I'm lost."

He stood in place, watching me, offering nothing.

"I don't understand you," I said, "—don't live here, don't speak the language, can barely breathe the air, what was the question?"

Dora took one step down toward me. "He asked you, awhile ago"—she pointed behind me to where we'd been—"to say what must he do."

I remembered. Right—weeks, years, miles back. And I'd offered banter, shirked a clear duty. I waited a moment to be entirely sure—that I knew a true answer, that I wanted to give it. I *knew* and not only wanted but needed to give it. My earlier joke about Last Words had hardened—a serious possibility. I was near some extreme. They seemed merely inconvenienced— Blix and Dora—delayed in their flight toward a smiling South. Oranges, cures, children rising around them. But I knew better. I gave it to her. "Kill you now."

She turned back to Blix as though he would obey me instantly and she must meet him, ready but calm.

He had heard me—I'd seen him flinch—but now he'd turned and started again. Four, five steps away.

She looked to me and said "How come?"

"Because you are dying this slowest death. Because he is planning to take you off from here, thinking he understands what you need and can use—when what's

got him trapped is your warm hole on cold bedsprings.
They grow on *trees*. More than half the world's got one
—and yours is cooling." I knew—as I said it—that it
meant no more to her than a Mozart aria and forgave
myself before I'd even finished. I *knew* it was that—an
aria of my own (well-built, self-pleased) that barely
concerned her; a soliloquy of rage simply flung at her as
the nearest ear. *I am not even cruel.*

But she stood and seemed to think. No more
backward checks on Blix—I could barely see him beyond her. Then she said "How about me waiting?"

"—Waiting?"

"Just till I die." She thumbed behind her, again as
to a place, a clear geographical destination, visible on
maps, toward which we would move if we moved again.

"When will that be?"

"Pretty soon"—no shrug, no smile; she was dealing
in facts.

"Who told you?"

She pointed, not looking—the Gallup light. "Hospital doctor."

"Sclerosis?"

She nodded.

"You may have years; it can take twenty years."

"I won't take 'em though."

"You'll stop it?" I said.

"Yep."

"When?"

She calculated. In the dark and with her so foreign, it was like—what?—witnessing an animal's deci-
sion. The stock analogies for primitive peoples—cats,
panthers, cougars. Are they thinking at all or in a state
of being as inviolate as bread?—that dense and pure. I

thought of rushing on her, splitting skull in my hands to trap this thought she was boring through now, a mole in loam—children crush pet fish to see what they hold.

She said "Let me wait."

"Sure," I said. "OK by me. I was just giving answers, just aiming to please."

She waited again but with no hint of thought. Now she was searching—my face, eyes, hands. She said "Then you."

She had skipped several steps in a human argument. I said "Me what?"

"You go on—do it now."

I meant to laugh but didn't. "Kill you?"

"Yep."

"Why me?"

"You good at it."

I waited, then looked round me—tracked snow, barbed wire, scattered brush ten yards away. I remembered her kinsman—no matches, no fire. I finally could laugh. "I forgot my tools."

"What you need?" she said. "I'm making it easy."

She was—I saw. Nothing so obvious as chin-back, throat taut; but in her silent breathing, her short birdbones, entirely destructible. She could not only have been easily killed here by hand with the little strength I had, but killed entirely—razed, no remains, all instantly dissolved to earth, thin air; or departed, bag and baggage, for her afterworld. I said "Wait; you can wait" and stepped to go.

She was in the path, not moving. "No. Now, you please."

I was ten inches from her. She was giving off cold,

not body heat but cold more intense than the night's
—waste from her burning. *A different animal.* I looked
again for Blix. Nothing. Gone. Past the crest of the
next hill. Two dogs began barking then. A quarter-mile
ahead—or five or at hand? Dogs? Coyotes? Wolves?
Navajo wolves? "Blix will do it," I said.

She nodded—"Slow."

"But you wanted that."

She waited. "Yep." Then she turned and led off.
No waiting for me. No squaw's place in line.

We moved toward the howling. Wherever, whatever, it was strengthening, nearing. I thought of Blix,
already torn and consumed and of us straining now in
every fiber to add the remains of ourselves to the feast
—as eaters or eaten? Cold suppers indeed.

She spoke as she moved—no pause, no looking
back, her breath completely adequate. "You think you
winning."

I heard it as a question, though her voice never
rose, and I quickly said "Yes."

"You ain't," she said.

It had been a stated fact—what I'd taken as question. The first fact she'd stated since the cause of her
illness, the snake touched in school. All the rest had
been shifting—lies, questions, half-jokes, trashy specu-
lations. (Who was she? Who was her father? Where
was her mother, her two alleged children? Who were
all those drunks and where had they vanished to?
Whose truck had that been? Was her name what she
claimed?—or what Blix had told me; she'd never said
her own name, certainly not mine.) I said "Dora?"

She didn't turn.

"Dora?"—again, louder. The howling could have

drowned me. Or the wires overhead. They were hum-
ming now steadily with an idiot force—feeding power
to whom? to start what engines? Or bearing what
voices, planning what? in what language?

No turn. But no quickening either, no fear or
flight. This girl, whoever, was holding ground—only
the ground was snow and was sliding beneath her as
she pumped on toward survival, effortlessly. (*She*
should be telling this—a calm winter's tale, cool pas-
toral, a day in the hills by purling streams, ample
breath, warming blood, obedient limbs.)

Speech was difficult again, simple breath. But I
said "I've won."

After three steps—"What?"

"—That I'm free now in my life, have what I
need."

"Need what?"

"*Room.*"

"You ain't got room?"

"—To live my life, work."

"What you mean by work?"

"I'm a writer, I write."

"What sort of writing?"

"Stories."

"What you going to tell them?"

"What I know—how I've won."

Another set of steps—"That's what you won?"

"All I tried to win."

She laughed—a soft luxurious laugh, unjogged by
her steps. "And you think you'll get it home?"

"With you helping," I said.

"I'm helping."

"How?"

"—Leading," she said.

She was. Toward what? "What's howling?" I said.

"Dogs."

"You sure?"

"Yep," she said.

"Whose?"

"Bekis," she said.

A name? A word? "You know him?"

Silence.

"He kin to you?"

Silence.

*They are not dogs. She is leading me to them—as I
sent Blix to them.* But I didn't feel more fear. Feeling
had quit. "Where is Blix?" I said.

"Who?"

"Blix," I said. "Blix, your friend."

Silence. But her head shook, clearly, side to side.

*What—and in what language—does she mean?
Where is Blix—and on whose side? Who are we now?
What do we become?* "OK. Lead," I said—as though
she had stopped or was losing heart, when she moved
like an engine, the perfect machine of my punishment,
fed by power that leaked from the wires now roaring
above us. For I was in punishment—I saw—to the
eyes. What would constitute the end?—death, release,
maiming? We were climbing a hill now, the first for a
mile. Surely it was the last screen between the dogs and
us—me. I dropped a little behind her, not from choice
or fear but necessity—something was failing. Or trying
to fail—every three or four steps, with a clear metal *tick*
a spot on my brain, on the left frontal lobe (I could
have found it with a needle, gouged it into action),
attempted to refuse, to halt me here. A soft fall in snow

warmer than I, sleep till they woke me. *They?*

The top of the hill. Moonlight flattened the fore-
ground beneath us. At our left—a quarter mile—the
single dark house I had seen at dusk, one sizable tree, a
parked truck, silvered. The dogs' home—Bekis's? Was
Blix there now? Intending what? With Dora's drunk
kin?—their drunk wife as leader?

No. She said "Wait."

I took the order, stopped, sucked loudly for air.

But she hadn't meant me. Her own steps continued. Her right hand extended quickly before her and
she said again "Wait." She was calling to a distant,
approaching figure—a man two hundred yards beyond
her.

Though she had not raised her voice, he obeyed.
Stopped, facing us. *Us?*—maybe only her. Or me.

I waited. Passive suffering. No ordeal at all nor
the charged aftermath but a death dumbly welcomed
—not even welcomed, *borne.* A guy with his frozen
balls strangulated, his penis retracted to a bloodless
little tit, takes death without a peep—from him or the
sky. Sorry; I waited.

But she went on; her meeting-place was *there,*
ahead, plotted where the man had been stopped and
stood. No question of *her* waiting now.

I was the waiter and scrambled toward her will.

Blix—having gone where, for what, since he left
us? Her last letter to him—*light to your life.* He
seemed baked there by light—moonlight, monstrous
cold cookery; unable to move or save himself, *willing* in
fact to accept this death so he might obey orders.
Punish me. Light to *my* life. There are things the dead
forbid, have *died* to forbid and—even dead—have am-

ple means to enforce.

She was six steps ahead now—I'd counted them off. She cast a shadow. I used her own call—"Wait." Mine was plea not command.

But she stopped, again signaled Blix to stay; then she came back to me. She waited a step away, downhill from me now.

It's her. The malignant part. No, the *just* part, at last. Whatever other senses and functions were failing, I saw that clearly. Registered. I opened my mouth (I had caught a second wind in my moments of rest and was nose-breathing quietly); thin frozen air rammed in. Something still fought to stop me. But I won and said "Pardon"—and intended it chiefly as question not gift.

She shook her head slowly, then giggled, stamped her sneakers.

She didn't know the word.

"I'm sorry," I said.

"OK" she said. She still was baffled. But not by my second word—simply by newness. She was twenty-two years old. No one had ever yet asked her forgiveness. Or offered it.

I thought I was dying—simply failing in my tracks —but I said "OK what?"

"OK we got to move." She pointed to the hogan —"Or he be mad."

He was. He tried to kill us—mad or afraid? I could understand anger—that Blix stood in moonlight on the road before his house (a hundred yards before) and waited for us or for Dora as she'd asked; that this world was not big enough for him, his dogs and us—but as his first shot fired, I consciously thought, "No fear, no fear. I'm not followed now—actually alone; what I've meant to be."

The bullet struck the snow six feet ahead of Dora. She was twenty yards from Blix.

I walked on in silence but I studied her for advice —my own reflex, exhausted as I was, was to hit the deck, proceed by crawling or sleep here and die. I thought, "The first shot ever fired at me." Then re-membered—"The second. Will there be a third? Will that one land?" I tried to care but couldn't.

Dora strode on as calmly as on Miami Beach; and the dogs at least had quieted, gun-shy, in terror.

So I tried to mimic her and managed at least *continuance*. I wondered only one thing and asked her as we moved through the trough of that shot—"You know him you said?"

She nodded, a silent "Yep."

Another shot. Still just ahead of Dora and a little beyond, only this much more conclusive than the last —that if he had a target, the bullseye was Dora or else he was wild and striking out blind. I remembered how tender, how *at-mercy* I'd felt last night, earlier today, and wondered why not now—with a crazed redskin pumping hot lead my way and I under moonlight brighter than some noons? But again I didn't, couldn't —no certainty of safety, no clear death-wish, but no reluctance to die—and when we reached Blix—Dora stopped three steps from him—he must have seen me smiling. I was too cold to know or to alter a muscle.

He looked past her to me and smiled—first since when?—and said "How are you now?"

"Dying happy," I said—I'd read my own state

backward from his grin.

"Why happy?" he said, not denying I was dying.

No answer came to me—not to that; I couldn't think. Yet happy I was, if being past fear and with all debts paid is a brand of happiness. I stepped up toward him, leaving Dora behind us.

Another shot, in my old tracks behind her.

"What's his problem?" I said.

"This is his," Blix said.

"She knows him," I said.

He had not looked to Dora since our present meeting but said to me quietly, "She may say she does."

The links in Blix's thought and speech were weak now as mine—like tramps in Beckett, all connectives dissolved by acid fatigue; or like Jesus and Mary, Jesus and Judas, all courtesy, all human ritual abandoned— for pure discourse, *intercourse* (intention, comprehension). One dog cranked up again—his master back asleep? his master dead, vanished? or waiting to draw an infallible bead? I stepped between Blix and him, as best I could figure. Did I think I was a shield?—and if so, shielding what? Blix's simple head and heart? For what?—a future of nursing Dora? stuffing bedpans to a paralyzing Indian for ten, twenty years in a filthy room? —Too tired to know. I had simply moved, acted, abandoned myself again to accident—or plan. To die together maybe, one bullet for both, Dora our survivor. What would Dora do? Stand a moment and look, then leave us to stiffen six miles from her truck (was it hers at all?) and walk straight forward in her socks and sneakers to Bekis's house (was Bekis a person?), join him there in the dark. Warmth, giggle, hump, sleep,

warmth. The wires overhead had quieted, were silent
—a safety blackout or mission accomplished?

Blix renewed his smile. "Why happy?" he said.

"I know," I said. "There are people like me."

"So what," he said—no question at the end.
"There are more like me."

"Should I go on smiling then? Or bellow? Or die?
Doc—prescribe! prescribe!"

"Just hush and breathe gently. You're getting *air*.
There's air to go round. Uncle Sam provides it for all us
white folks, even out here—just a small service charge;
we'll bill you in April. Colored don't use it." He smiled
again, breathed deeply, a demonstration—that this air,
a frigid blade thin enough to pare cells, was the warm-
est stoutest drink at a good day's end.

I was better. I nodded "Look. You left us," I said.
"Why were you headed back?—just now when we saw
you, the top of that hill."

"I can hear the road. I was coming to tell you."
His arms stayed down, too tired to point; but his head
ducked backward.

So he could. So could I. Above the dogs, the still-
silent wires and despite the fact that the airport
light still searched *there* beyond us, unpassed, uncap-
tured—the wheels of cars. There was another world.
This one. Ours joined it. Waiting, reachable, if not
engaged in rescue. I asked Blix still—"Why did you
come back?"

"To tell you to hurry."

"I can't."

"You'll have to. Basketball traffic's what you're
hearing now, two miles ahead. Game over in Zuni.
When the last fan's passed on his way to Gallup—for-

get it; road closed; we'd have to walk till dawn. Twenty
more miles."

Dora took three steps—obedience—then stopped
beyond Blix and looked back, waiting.

The dogs were asleep or dead or had got her family
scent.

Blix moved in on me, took my elbow, pulled me
toward him—the direction of safety.

Oh Jesus I'm safe. "I can't," I said. (I had been
safe here; why depart for the world?)

He still was smiling—so now was Dora. "We can't
tote you."

"I don't ask that," I said.

"Then why are you smiling?"

I felt that I knew, that if they would wait—post-
pone their precious lives, say, twenty seconds till I
organized my heart, lungs, freed my dry tongue—I
could say it for them here in a line so lucid, so instantly
permanently usable as to constitute recompense for all
my family's damage, hers and mine—paid in full now
to Blix Cunningham and the girl he'd chosen (whatever her name), to Atso and Neely, Mae Clain, the
apple-brandied drunks, and paid where I'd won it: on a
lethal little sideroad near Remnant Mesa under Navajo
guns, an unfiltered moon, seven thousand feet in the
air above my home. But it gobbed my throat (just the
words, short breath; no hand at my larynx now, spectral
or human). So when Blix pulled again—on my wrist
now, still holding me, my pulse warming under him—
I moved off beside him; and when I could speak (knew
it all, controlled my means), the paved road stretched
there clearly before us (taillights, heaters—*my* goal)
and Blix had run ahead again to flag salvation; so I

said it to myself (which is to say, to you) since Dora lacked the English words to hear me, even—"You know every answer now, or all you need. What we are —we three, the name of our spectacle: *Happy Though Breathing.* And beyond this night—how I caused it, how I didn't. Why she did it, why I'll never know. Why I'm glad and smiling. *Glad* despite my begging pardon, two miles back, under force but not from guns —because, look, she has *given* it, an act of oblivion. I am both free and working. I have forced you this far. You know this story, know all I know once I've told you this last—she is dead and dumb. Hammer-dead. Her name was Beth."

REYNOLDS PRICE

Born in Macon, North Carolina in 1933, Reynolds Price attended North Carolina schools and received his Bachelor of Arts degree from Duke University. As a Rhodes Scholar he studied for three years at Merton College, Oxford, receiving the Bachelor of Letters. In 1958 he returned to Duke where he teaches for one term each year in the Department of English. There he began and completed A Long and Happy Life, *which was published in 1962 and received the award of the William Faulkner Foundation for a notable first novel. In 1961 he again traveled to England where he worked for a year at the stories which were published in 1963 as* The Names and Faces of Heroes. *His second novel* A Generous Man *appeared in 1966; his third* Love and Work, *in 1968. He has read and lectured at a number of American universities but continues to live and write in Orange County, North Carolina.*